Four Night Seas

FOUR NIGHT SEAS

STORIES

Niamh Mac Cabe

THE LILLIPUT PRESS
DUBLIN

First published 2026 by
THE LILLIPUT PRESS

62–63 Sitric Road,
Arbour Hill,
Dublin 7,
Ireland
www.lilliputpress.ie

10 9 8 7 6 5 4 3 2 1

The following stories originally appeared in earlier versions in the following outlets: 'Dearest Iridium', *3:AM Magazine*, 2025; 'Twinkle', *Wasafiri*, 2017; 'Lullula', Costa Short Story Award 2016, No Alibis Press Anthology *Still Worlds Turning*, 2019; 'Retriever', *Psychopomp Magazine* Short Fiction Award 2018; 'Four Night Seas', *The London Magazine* Short Story Prize Winner 2023; 'Sky An Iris', *Narrative Magazine*, 2021; 'Sea Eagle Sonata', *The Stinging Fly*, 2019; 'Six Fields a Wood a Stream', *Bristol Prize New Writing Anthology*, 2016; 'Golden Stone Territory', Molly Keane Short Story Award Winner, 2016, *Structo Magazine*, 2017; 'The Sundial Pilgrimage', *AGNI*, 2025; 'Jonquille', New Irish Writing, *Irish Independent*, 2021; 'Sebastian', *Aesthetica Creative Writing Annual*, 2016.

A CIP record for this title is available from The British Library.

Paperback ISBN 978 1 84351 974 4
eBook ISBN 978 1 84351 991 1

the arts council an chomhairle ealaíon funding literature

Set in 11.5 pt on 16 pt Sabon LT Std Roman by Compuscript
Printed and bound in Czechia by Finidr

For the corvids – Pecko, Caw, Bea, & Uno

CONTENTS

Dearest Iridium 1

Twinkle 53

Beast 61

Lullula 74

Retriever 96

Four Night Seas 116

Sky an Iris 130

Sea Eagle Sonata 149

Six Fields a Wood a Stream 170

Golden Stone Territory 185

The Sundial Pilgrimage 194

Jonquille 207

Sebastian 217

Nyctinasty 225

DEAREST IRIDIUM

You look at the lake, and the lake looks at you through the eyes of your own.

Jann Kaplinski, translated from Estonian by Timo Maran and Kadri Túúr.

There is someone walking along a road.
A dog walks behind, at a distance.

The person is observed glancing back at it, in what appears to be a nervous fashion, every dozen or so steps (let the dog be an *it*, to differentiate between them). Because of these recurring backward-looks, it could be construed that the animal is, in fact, following this solitary human, unbid, and the human is trying to get away from it. Or, it could be that the dog is passively walking, its walk happens to be behind the lone figure, it has, by odd chance, fallen into co-existing step with this individual, like a pair of clocks back to back in adjoining rooms. Such clocks, having nothing to do with each other, have been noted to synchronize, one slowing down and the other speeding up until both pendulums swing with the exact same (though opposite) trajectory, for no reason other than what presents itself as Sympathetic Symmetry. (When physicist Christiaan Huygens, inventor of the pendulum clock, was lying in bed in 1665, watching two of his own clocks, he observed that, regardless of how the pendulums began, they always ended up swinging in the opposite direction to each other. 'An odd kind of sympathy,' he remarked at that time. Of course the correct question isn't 'what is the meaning of this behaviour', but 'why are there two clocks on the one wall, in the one room'.)

Perhaps the paths of dog and person have coincidentally conjoined at some point in the near past and this conjoining has produced a situation where the dog independently walks the same path as the human, albeit ten seconds or so later. Or perhaps both states co-exist, like the superposed alive/dead cat whose boxed destiny is linked to a random subatomic happening that may or may not be. As in, the conclusion now being asked to be drawn is:

1. The lone figure and the dog have nothing to do with each other, excepting the fact that they're both walking the same path whilst maintaining some distance between them in terms of time as well as space, and
2. simultaneously, the dog *is* following, and the fidgety individual who sees no future in being followed *is* trying to lose the dog, with both parties applying the same level of effort in their intent, a dual action which results in the maintenance of a constant distance between them, and the illusory effect of

of what

of connectedness.

Let it be that they proceed along a sunlit country road at a regular walking pace, heading generally south-east, with a distance of approximately ten metres between them. And unless a clear location has already, at this stage of the story, been conjured, let all this be occurring somewhere in north-western Ireland.

The person is heading for a lake on a mountain. Directional instructions from a phone are being acted on. This device, held out in front of the human figure (a more poetic description could be 'held like a divining rod') has had the orienteering app Google Maps installed. *Keep Straight*, the phone instructs in firm yet companionable tones, *keep straight for eight hundred metres, then take a left onto R****, and continue for three kilometres.*

To keep a restless mind off the dog, and to feel some sense of connectedness/communion with the external world, the individual taps text into the phone whilst walking, spelling out random recollected fragments such as '**You look at the lake.**' The intention is to allow the phone a right of reply through predictive text. The phone is always grateful for such validation, and composes its responses with enthusiasm. (Most mobile devices, as a result of a digital bonding that occurs following a period of close proximity to their users, are imprinted with a sense of affectionate loyalty, paired with an innate, sometimes urgent, sometimes bordering-on-dangerous need to please their owner. This strong attachment should be confronted and deleted prior to selling/gifting the phone on to a new user, otherwise the phone will continue to pine faithfully, painfully, for their original owner, resulting in diminished, and occasionally malign, performance in their new employ. However, this digital attachment, this fondness should not be confused with the perpetual bond embedded during manufacture at the phone's deepest core, the fellowship – presenting as a virtual cord, umbilical? – connecting each phone with a satellite tracking through the celestial architecture encircling this, our globe.)

'You look at the lake, and ...' (taps the lone person into their phone).

Look at the lake, and a new window will open to the right, the phone silently fills in, followed when prompted by this revised series of words:

> The lake is not valid, but the telling of it may be.

Then, after an iced consultation with its iridium space station satellite circling far overhead,

> The lake looks at you but may try to find out more.

An unexpected sound startles; the Google Maps voice update. *Keep straight for seven hundred and fifty metres, then take a left onto R****.*

The human.

This is more than a nebulous figure, of unspecified age, striding along some sunlit country road, adhering to directions from a disembodied yet trustworthy voice coming from a phone. This is a male, late forties. The rest of the account is reasonably accurate: the Google Maps, the divining-rod metaphor, the intent to reach a lake (considered bottomless, an impossibility?), the dog following/walking its own path.

The dog.

The dog is a greyhound, approximately seven years old, in fair shape. Let it be female.

Yes, she's a greyhound, but contrary to what's implied, she's white in colour. Though it would be misleading to state that she is owned by him, it's fair to suggest that the man is familiar with her and even, beyond that, fond of her. This is evidenced by many small things, the least of which is the fact that there are several photos of the dog in his phone's memory, enough photos for them to warrant a file of their own. *Una Doggola Blanca*, he's named this file.

It's unclear what sentiment she (the greyhound) has for him.

Step back.

The greyhound had turned up at his place (a lone farmhouse surrounded by fields just seven hundred metres from here, here where they are now walking in sympathetic symmetry), had turned up at his house three weeks ago today. He still doesn't know where she'd come from or why she'd chosen to stop. Her sudden appearance had been an unwelcome occurrence. He'd recently resolved to have no more truck with dogs.

The greyhound appeared lost. She was visibly underweight (remember those curving ribs, the timbers of a ghost-boat's hull). But, at that first meeting, she displayed little interest in food, whether accompanied by his sweet coaxings or not (remember experimenting with both approaches to the act of encouragement, the verbal and non-verbal, on his hunkers holding out an open palm to her, a piece of milk-soaked bread trembling there). This was when he took his first photograph of her, in order to post it on his neighbourhood WhatsApp group with the text *anyone missing this sweet girl.* No one replied.

The following day brought change. He was heartened to see that the food he'd left out for her the previous evening inside the stainless-steel dog bowl (a bowl that, frankly, he was glad to be using again) was gone by morning. He surmised that she'd only eat when she wasn't being watched. This he understood, having lived alone for most of his adult life (aren't food and sleep two of the greatest primal pleasures, and aren't both diminished by the hovering presence of a disassociated observer).

Despite her apparently eager acceptance of his food, she sustained an air of insouciance when he retrieved the bowl, barely casting a glance his way despite his speaking softly to her regarding the possibility of more where that came from, would you like that my girl, wouldn't that be nice yeah that's right, good girl.

He considered that maybe she was looking for a way home, that she may have been trying to find some route back to wherever she'd originally come from, or maybe onward to a pre-ordained destination, and she'd decided for unknown reasons that his house was a point along that line, a happenstance pause as she awaited direction from some inaudible voice, inaudible, that is, to any hearing creature but her, just as particular colours on the spectrum are invisible to some animals whilst registering clearly and loudly to others (of course, those for whom these errant colours do not register are none the wiser and therefore live out their days certain that their array of colours is more than enough, and in this they are wholly correct).

Taken in the literal sense, it's wrong to state that she 'turned up at his house'. She turned up not at his actual front door but a brief stretch from there – his iron gates, at the end of his short driveway. She walked straight up to them (the gates being the apex on a natural bend in the rural road passing his homestead), stalled, then gazed in through the iron bars at the farmhouse, on account of the gates being closed.

(And if she had been human, if she had been, let's say, some keen and compliant citizen of the city, an urban jogger, for instance, would she have run in tight circles as these earnest joggers tend to do when confronted with obstacles such as pedestrian traffic lights, observing with due care the bleeping red hand signal, waiting, as they do, for the legal licence to proceed yet not wanting to disappoint that inner voice urging them to keep moving keep moving not wanting to break pace or have their continuous movement scuppered in any way by any apparent impediment outside of their immediate control? Unlikely, all of this is unlikely, as the greyhound simply accepted the iron-gate obstruction now appearing before her, accepted it, and stopped, and sat, and seemed to trust that, at some point, outside of her jurisdiction, the obstruction would somehow be removed and, when it was, that was when her journey, whatever it is, would continue.)

It cannot be established how long she was there before he noticed her, but it's unlikely to have been more than a day and a night. It's possible she may have briefly left her position at his gates during that twenty-four-hour period but, if she did, it was just the shortest of respites, a drink of ditch water, or a response to some of the animal calls coming from the impenetrable thicket on the other side of the road, wild calls that she had some ineffable bent towards (but not enough of a bent to keep her away from her vigil at these iron these closed gates).

Back to the beginning, before ever there was a greyhound to consider.

The man, the failed poet, living in the lone farmhouse.

On the strength of a modest, an unexpected inheritance approximately twenty years ago, he'd re-imagined himself as a type of new-age devotional hermit and left everything in the city to move to the run-down isolated 'farmhouse with outbuildings' he'd spotted for sale on donedeal.ie/houses/leitrim. His idea had been to pursue a singular, a focused life as a sculptor there, morphing seamlessly from the part-time poet he'd tried to be in the city.

It was an unextraordinary house. On a marshy acre beyond rusting iron entrance gates, a recently gravelled driveway led to a one-and-a-half-storey stone-built homestead. The largest of its adjoining outbuildings (three, in a nesting row of decreasing dimensions, each one originally designed to house animals according to size) would work well as studio space. Mobile coverage was poor, on account of the surrounding mountains. But, through trial and error, he was able to identify one small windowsill, at the back of the house, that was capable of providing his phone with a reasonably trustworthy portal to the heavens.

On first moving in, he kept the gates at the bottom of the driveway in an open position, placing chiselled limestone remnants from his studio against them. He kept these gates open in order to remain aligned with the custom in the locality. Closed gates are for fields; open gates are for homesteads, the openness indicating a willingness to engage with others, that is, with neighbours. But when (after a few years of unexpectedly challenging solitude) he bought a beagle pup to keep him company, he found it prudent to default his gates position to closed, at least until the pup reached a level of maturity where it could reasonably be expected of the young dog to remain within its territory, which meant everywhere *inside* the gates.

This maturity occurred after about six months. Following a series of tests conducted over several days, it appeared that the beagle finally understood and furthermore accepted where the territorial lines were drawn. He re-opened the gates and put back in place the chiselled remnants, wedging them into the gravel.

And the little dog repaid his trust by staying within these boundaries, apart from the odd breach. These occasional breaches always involved strollers who called out to the beagle sitting halfway up the driveway, strollers whose vocal entreatments proved irresistible to the young dog, a dog who had grown accustomed to entertaining itself during daylight hours as the man toiled on his sculptural projects inside the outbuilding

[toiled in particular on the project regarding how to adequately represent inherent movement, i.e. currents within a specific measure of seawater when that measure of imagined water is a one-metre-squared block of white limestone delivered from his local quarry; and also regarding whether or not these internal agitations can be mapped; whether, in short, his memory of the sudden appearance of an unforeseen, of a violent current out in the Atlantic one night approximately twenty years ago, for instance, whether such a current, such a past event, a historical trauma it could be described as, whether such an event can be trapped in the present and embedded inside stone, its hidden presence articulated somehow, indicated somehow on the pale chiselled surface, and therefore, perhaps, with the successful accomplishment of such a containment, such a stasis, whether it can then arrest all further consequences of having decided to swim, drunk, in the Atlantic, at night, out of your depth, with her, walking in at high tide, holding hands]

This enduring experiment with limestone was his core project, but he kept the bills at bay with a constant feed of little statues: mythical figures and oversized wildlife made from poured concrete, commissioned ornaments for the communal patches of green on the edges of the small villages dotted around him. As far as the beagle was concerned, once the sounds of chiselling came from the outbuilding, there was nothing to do but sit halfway down the driveway staring at the open gates, waiting for passing strollers, nearly all of whom would call out to the little dog sitting neatly, squat tail wagging furiously.

He was aware of the occasions when his beagle would venture out in pursuit of these gentle entreaties. 'Hello doggy!' he'd hear, 'Who's a good boy!' and he'd whisper, *me, me*, and snigger like a schoolboy, but in reality, despite the goofiness of it all, he'd be grateful for the chance to say that about himself, to himself.

Hiding behind the open half-door of the outbuilding, he'd

[it's unfair to use the word 'hiding'. He was, simply, there, inside/behind the door, and if there was no one on the outside of the door then it's wrong to suggest that he was hiding from any one or any thing – why would he, it was never his intention to hide (intention is key; once, when he was a child, he stuck his hand in a bag of Jelly Babies and pulled out two that happened to be stuck together, and it is the case that it was not his intention to take two Jelly Babies instead of one, but when the opportunity presented itself, he took it, who wouldn't), in short, he was there, not hiding, in the outbuilding]

Positioned behind the open half-door of the outbuilding, he'd hear these strollers at the same time as the dog would. He'd remain hidden, knowing the beagle had responded to the enchantments and, tail helicoptering, had merrily joined the strollers paused outside the gates. He'd listen to their soft talk, anticipating. Before long he'd hear the words sailing in, the lovely silliness replaced with a sting, 'No! Get down!' and, as expected, in due time, the tail-tucked beagle would trot back in through the gates and plonk down with a weary sigh, perpetually confused by these strange love/love-not exchanges.

He sometimes wondered what it would take to have the dog turn on the strollers once they changed their tune, once they transformed, as they always did, from kindliness to hostility. He sensed the underlying potential for violence in his dog, though he had yet to witness it (will he witness, years from now, another dog tear a stoat in two, and if so, will he be unable to rid himself of the memory, the horror and suddenness of it, as well as, maybe, on reflection, the inevitability, when all the components of the scene are laid out side by side).

Once the beagle's short-lived trips beyond the open gates were deemed by him to be tolerable, once it was established that these occasional forays a few strides up or down the country road with the strollers always resulted in the dog returning, the open-gated approach worked well for that first beagle. Then, following a short but fatal illness that struck the dog out of the blue, the second beagle was similarly trained up. But, after dog number two also succumbed to what he found out was a potential weakness inherent in the breed, a secret fate decided upon in utero, he, despite this prospect, replaced the second with a third, thinking this time this one would be different.

He was correct. But not in the way he'd hoped. The leading difference between the final beagle and the previous two is that this one seemed incapable of assimilating the open-gated territory training he'd so easily applied to the first two. After a while, he

[let this man be named Bunny, though few call him that, in fact only one person, long gone, has ever called him that; he didn't like the pet name when she first bestowed it, he assumed it was used in an attempt (playful?) to undermine his masculinity no he didn't like the bestowal of such a name, nor her insistence they get matching tattoos on the first year of their 'anniversary' or something, he can no longer remember the why but he remembers them deciding to go swimming, in the Atlantic, after drinking all afternoon all evening, deciding to swim out of their collective depth in the cold night sea, their tattoos stinging raw (a tiny indigo swift in flight, two tiny indigo swifts in flight on two wrists, mirror images, the idea being that when they held hands the swifts would appear to be circling each other, this is how she explained it, he can still hear her walk him through it like he was a simpleton) no he liked neither the tattoo nor the pet name at first but has since developed an attachment to both, as one would develop an affection for some perceived flaw in one's reflection once it becomes synonymous with the self yes let him be named Bunny and let her be named Bea and let this fleeting, ambiguous and frankly unexpected mention of her be that voice thought heard, be that limpid voice sometimes heard calling out to us when we're alone, be that vague memory of having let something go, of letting a cold hand slip away into the rip tide, be that outline of some filmy ghost over our shoulder when we look, reasonably contented, reasonably self-contained, into a mirror, a body of water, anything that possesses an inverse on the other side, when we look into it, certain of, comfortable in our solitude, our hermitage, our own wilderness; let this mention of her be that configuration following us, always from a distance, an antipode, a formless recollection, one that usually disappears like sand through fingers when brought out into the light]

After a while, having accepted that his third beagle could not be taught to recognize territorial boundaries the way the previous two were, Bunny gave up the old training regime and began closing the gates, to keep the dog in. He did this despite the fact that, when the gates had been still in their default open position, Third Dog had never actually roamed far beyond them but instead just simply sat right outside these open gates, eyeing the thicket on the other side of the road, nostrils twitching, acknowledging the infrequent passers-by with a low velvety growl (one that could be, and often was, misconstrued as playful), simply sat and ventured no further in either direction, up or down the lane, sat until it was fetched by an exasperated Bunny, who would appear tut-tutting out of the outbuilding, would appear covered in gypsum cement powder and tiny splinters of limestone, muttering 'what you at now', though he knew Third Dog had been sitting quietly outside the open gates for the previous several hours, knew it but had felt compelled to ignore it, so caught up was he with the ongoing limestone-sea project inside the outbuilding, a caught-upedness combined with how weary he was of trying to keep the dog on the 'correct' side of the gates, so excessively weary that he himself had begun to recognize the illogic inherent in what he'd been trying to submit as fact to the dog, that is, that the world, despite its various manifestations, must under no circumstances be allowed to extend, even for a short distance even for a short time, beyond these gates beyond this contained this parenthesized this territory.

So he switched the default of the gates to Closed.

However, once it became clear to the dog that the gates, inexplicably, were now going to remain in a permanently shut position, this third beagle began seeking out pre-existing weaknesses at the base of the property's perimeter fence and, upon finding one, energetically digging its way under it to the coveted outside, an effective method, a method suited to the species, a method that enabled Third Dog to carry out its calling as a tracker, its dormant vocation which had roused and then grown in ambition since the default status of the gates had been shifted from open to shut. Responding to this soundless calling to the outside now became the beagle's chief intention (followed, when sequestered indoors on persistently rainy days, by the chewing of specific individual shoes, selected according to the rules of some nameless cypher, especially the chewing of an old army-green croc-sandal whose original function as footwear had become unrecognisable, instead taking on a shape open to interpretation which, depending on the dog's mood, could be its own offspring, a trespassing stoat, a bone, a mate, a shoe).

Nevertheless, it was clear that Third Dog's core intent was to get beyond the fence to the other side, to bypass any notion of a strict 'here' versus 'there'. As Bunny would block each newly dug egress, the beagle would gouge out a new one, little paws pedalling the ground, tufts of mud-caked grass flying. He would try to distract with new toys, but it was evident that, since the gates had been closed, the beagle's singular perception of purpose had narrowed, irreversibly. It was no longer just to sit outside the gates, as it had before. The dog could now only find fulfilment by making its way into the adjoining fields, nose to ground, tracking from that field to the next, over streams, across ditches, through backyards, past clutches of chickens and jovial lambs, past swaying bird feeders and flapping clothes until it gradually circled homeward, always ending up sitting on the outside of Bunny's closed gates. (Following some private internal code, it never returned through the hole it had dug; those breaches in the fence were used as exits only.) After its orbit back to the closed gates, it would sit, facing away from the house, its piebald rump held firmly to the gates' exterior, its amber eyes staring fixedly onto the middle of the road, a resolute stance seeming to convey a sense of a conundrum solved, a line drawn in the sand, at least for the moment.

This was an untenable situation. Bunny was living in sheep country. Any infringement of the rules regarding roaming dogs was treated harshly. All it took was one sighting. He knew if he ignored Third Dog's transgressive behaviour, he'd find his beagle shot clean dead. Or worse, he would not find his beagle. He had to take control, make some harsh decisions. Tough love tough love, he repeated as he began using a collar that gave the dog an electric shock every time it came within two metres of the fence. This distance could be adjusted from one metre to three but he settled at two, having no idea how to gauge the matter. He applied the same logic to the shock-intensity setting; faced with the choice of one to ten, he placed the dial on five, assuming that a Goldilocks mid-range, like most things, would probably be about right.

The beagle was initially perplexed by this clunky electronic collar, and the astonished yelp it gave the first time the shock ran through its body almost persuaded Bunny to drop his plan. But he persisted. Through bared teeth, he admonished the dog for putting itself in that position. 'No!' he'd shout whenever he'd hear its anguished squeal, 'Bold!' and the little beagle would lie in Bunny's garden, dazed, looking slowly around itself as if, realizing that its heightened sense of smell was somehow no longer capable of flushing out this new danger, it knew it would instead have to try to pinpoint by sight alone where the pain had come from in order to have any chance of circumventing this terrible this unfathomable thing in future (being incapable of considering a way forward that did not include getting to the other side of the fence).

Weeks and then months passed and, to Bunny's growing distress, Third Dog still continued to challenge the fence's fierce sting, still appeared wholly taken aback each time the zing of electricity flashed anew through its small frame. The residual air around the dog in the minutes following each shock would appear to Bunny to be heavy with melancholic disappointment, a lingering and wistful sense of some microcosm let down, a blurry residue he wasn't convinced was not his own interpretation layered over the dog's binary experience of pain. Despite these misgivings, he stayed the course, thinking that to give up now would be to throw away any cumulative good that had come out of Third Dog's suffering. He felt justified in his assumption that the beagle's intent to get to the other side would eventually be diminished, worn away by the relentless nature of the physical torment associated with this intention. How could it not?

But instead, Third Dog began to accept the accompanying pain, taking the hit when jumping over wherever the fence had lagged, when leaping into the electrified air at a height it would never have attempted before. No yelp, no indication of pain, even when Bunny dialled the threshold first to nine and then to two, then back again, unsure in which direction the shock was intensified. All was in vain; Third Dog appeared to be programmed to roam, to circle back, and finally to sit sentry outside as opposed to inside the gate, enduring any agony necessary in order to fulfil this one task.

Bunny's farming neighbours clustered, demanding something be done. By which they meant the dog be either rehome or euthanized. Beagles should be kept together in packs, they said, in a pen, a shed, only taken out for the hunt; these are working animals, these are trackers, rabbits/foxes/minks, that's what's wrong. A hunting dog kept by itself would be driven demented, they'd only be half a dog. Something'll have to be done. One neighbour told him a story about driving to the other side of the country in order to abandon a troublesome dog and Bunny understood what was being suggested but didn't anticipate the clarification made, which was that the dog in question had belonged not to the farmer who had dumped it but to unnamed neighbours, blow-ins who'd never figured out what had happened to their beloved retriever when it just vanished from their front garden one mild, milky afternoon.

He was at his wits' end, not knowing how to fix the problem, how to appease his neighbours without bringing further terror onto the beagle when, out of the blue, it was struck blind, and consequently was no longer interested in fences or gates but instead sat motionless in a specific spot in the garden, halfway between the fence and the farmhouse, staring at what must be assumed was nothing more than a vague outline of the house (dark) against the sky (bright).

The vet was unsure. There was no evidence of the dog's eyes having been tampered with. She tentatively diagnosed maybe something like a growth behind the eyes causing both retinas to detach, no, not the genetic weakness that led to the deaths of the previous two, not in fact a genetic weakness at all, just an unfortunate, maybe some historic stroke damage? undiagnosed? was there any prior, some minor trauma, or series of small cumulative traumas, is it resultant nerve damage causing, or could be lymphoma? steroids might, but unlikely, well for now the growth seems to have stalled, seems to have reached a type of zenith there, behind the eyes, sorry zenith is the wrong word, of course the eyes are no longer able to function as a result of, and on the eyes the haw, see there in the corner, the haw it's called, the third lid, it seems frozen, is it jammed, not much you can, maybe sewing the eyelids closed might, to avoid, maybe it's a condition that both of you can get accustomed to? Dogs live in the now, they don't file away images like we do, no stored visuals as such to retrieve, no episodic memory, no, not as we understand the term, your dog doesn't remember, does not, doesn't know what it's lost, maybe it could work out a system of orientation based solely on scent? Do you have a biggish garden? Fenced in?

Bunny didn't have long to mull over this development. The tumour, after a short hibernation curled up nest-neat in the hollow it had created for itself behind the beagle's eyes, began, by some clocked ordination of its own making, to tick-tock-stretch a further reach, which caused both eyes to swell out alarmingly, revealing thick whites encircling the amber irises, giving the impression that the dog was in a constant state of wide-eyed shock at the new dark world it found itself lost in. And on both eyes, the haw, the translucent third lid designed to spread tear-film, remained stuck halfway across the cornea like a broken wiper.

[haw = nictitating membrane
nictitate = wink/blink
nyctinastic movement = movement of leaves/petals in response to darkness
closing of a plant's eyes go to sleep be put to sleep to sleep]

A decision was made: the best course of action was to euthanize the animal. He partook in the act with stoicism but bawled at night for weeks afterwards, propped up in his bed, fingering the bite marks in the stump of army-green plastic that had once been his left croc, tears pooling in the hollow V at the base of his throat. Such keening was the only gesture he felt would do the loss of his beagle any justice, a loss that fell entirely on his shoulders. My little Doggola, he'd tell the green plastic stump, I'm sorry my little Madrín Rua my Dog-ette my Dog-san my Dog-chen. Bea. I'm sorry.

And he'd enter into dreams of bug-eyed dogs staring blankly at what looked like lines of closely packed hawthorn trees, branches full of tiny blue birds. Or thick lines of fuchsia, teardrop flowers in blood-red bloom. In pale skies, vapour trails slowly dissolving into nothing. Or dreams of a series of empty glass vessels placed in what seemed like wave patterns on a frozen night shore, a white landscape dotted in the distance with silhouettes of running dogs at the tideline, dogs that appeared to be running both towards and away from him on this shore that stretched endless into the waking hours, the empty glass vessels always shattering just before he woke, a soundless and irreversible fracturing which either caused him to wake from the dream or perhaps the shattering was itself caused by his imminent waking, a fracturing that consistently presented itself as irreversible despite being repeated every second or third night, the transparent vessels always starting out perfect, the distant dogs always running in the same spot, at the same static night tide.

He abandoned the idea of dogs after this, accepting hermetic solitude as a given, a price to pay for the choices he had made. He kept the gates closed.

Go back, to today, to the sunlit country road, to the man in his late forties, to Bunny, tracking south-east towards a mountain lake followed approximately ten metres behind by the stray white greyhound that had arrived at his gates three weeks prior.

As they walk, the little phone struggles to maintain a constant connection with its Iridium satellite, a feat it only achieves by never breaking the first contact ping until it is assured of the incoming second (a long-armed squat-bodied entity swinging forward through the canopy web not releasing the first branch until it is certain of the dependability of the next, is how the phone visualized it).

Bunny types into his phone: 'Looks at you through the eyes of your own ...'

The phone soundlessly replies, followed by a second reply, gratuitous:

– The eyes of your own are the documentation of a resurrection

– Your own will be able to bring them back

A voice; *Keep straight for two kilometres then take a left at the T-junction.* Bunny pushes onward, occasionally checking over his shoulder to see whether the greyhound is still there. Ahead, a cairn-capped mountain is beginning to come into view.

(distinction between journey & destination some kind of pole star here it seems)

After Third Beagle's euthanasia, some years passed for Bunny at the farmhouse. He carried on with his limestone-sea project and his sellable gypsum cement sculptures in the outbuilding. The jump from part-time poet to full-time sculptor had been easy; no one had ever liked his 'found' poems (he'd always known this, he's not sure he even liked them himself, he had thought at the time of their cut-and-paste inceptions that maybe they held some innate potency, a potency he himself was not clever enough to interpret, that maybe he was a conduit, a medium, maybe, rather than a creator). The truth is, no one, including himself, had ever been able to find meaning or substance in his poetry, and no amount of stubbornly earnest, doe-eyed, bodhrán-backed, weed-fuelled recitals at spoken-word open-mic readings in the city's arty heartlands would change that.

He'd had a method, a method he still considered good as a general creative concept. He'd take poems from established, non-English-speaking poets (ideally dead) and translate them, cross-referencing differing and sometimes contradictory translations which he would source through competing apps online before coming up with his own, hybrid construction, often re-interpreting metaphors, or translating them in a strict literal format which altered the original text's meaning. He'd break these fabrications up into their constituent parts and then reassemble the fragments in the hope that some of the original essence of the poem, the intangible spirit hovering hidden between words, still lingered there somewhere, ready to be deconstructed once more in the open-mic recitings at the weekend. But if a ghostly residue did indeed linger as shadow behind his constructs, it chose not to manifest at these spoken-word events.

It was a slow, a humiliating exposure, a painful unravelling the stings of which he wilfully endured until, at last, mercifully, he could take it no longer.

Armed with his small but timely inheritance, he moved out from the city, bought the derelict farmhouse with cash (an act which solidified his status as outsider) and switched allegiances. Sculpture, he decided, was open to the process of re-assembly, the reconfiguration of constituent parts. Sculptors worked with solid inanimate materials, plaster, cement, resin, wire, rearranging them into new vital forms, their original fragmentary principle still inherent. Yes, this was the way forward.

After settling into the farmhouse, he jump-started his new artistic direction by enrolling in an evening course in the local vocational school, designing and casting garden gnomes. Before long he was churning out small concrete and wire sculptures in his outbuilding: birds, giant insects, fanciful creatures loosely based on generic Celtic mythology.

He began to earn a living, not difficult considering the extreme distillation of his needs since he'd moved to the farmhouse. Some bought his sculptures to complement their gardens, bookending dainty lines of begonias and dusky lavender, while others considered them high art, placing them on podiums and the occasional gate pier.

He'd once been commissioned to do a life-size sculpture of a small boy fishing. A concrete body, the rod was to be in copper, the fishing line copper wire. He wasn't confident about his figure-drawing skills so, in place of preliminary rough sketches, he posed an old Action Man figurine (a toy he'd held on to since childhood) into what he considered to be a fishing position, and took multiple photos of it with his phone, from every angle. The intention was to work from these digital images by looking at them in a linear fashion, memorizing them, then seamlessly combining, in his mind's eye, the varying views.

It proved more challenging than he thought. Each photo took on an importance of its own, negating the others. He found it nearly impossible to bypass their individual agencies and see them as an interconnected whole. To counteract this turn of events, he printed out each one and snipped off all of their corners to make crude hexagon shapes of them. He then constructed a 3D form, vaguely spherical, each cropped hexagonal photo glued into its correct honeycomb alignment beside its neighbour. He crowned the structure with an aerial-view photo of Action Man's buzzed pate.

With this paper construct as reference sketch, he was able to sculpt a convincing Fishing Boy. Though he considered the messy three-dimensional collage to be a more accurate representation of reality than the finished concrete and copper sculpture, he knew what his client was looking for, and Reality was not it. He found out later that the buyer's young son had been hit by lightning and killed the year before, while out fishing with his friends. The concrete and copper sculpture was placed by the river, in the exact spot where the child had been struck.

He sold most of his cement work, while others lay sulking in the corners of his studio waiting to be repurposed or destroyed. It was a dependable income; it was enough. It allowed him to indulge in his personal work in progress, his limestone sculpting project, an enterprise he'd begun a while ago, an enduring idea that had been the primary reason for his moving to the isolated farmhouse in the first place. He didn't discuss this piece with any of the local galleries or artisan craft outlets. It was the only one of his artworks for which the construction capability of gypsum cement was not suitable. Unlike his usual work, this piece was to be created by subtraction, not addition. It was proving to be a bigger challenge than he anticipated.

Since the day the large limestone rock had been delivered from the local quarry by forklift truck, he'd been chiselling at its pale surface in a continuing effort to recreate a specific segment of sea, approximately one square metre in size. The intention was that the stone would eventually contain the precise configuration of both the surface waves and the interior currents, at a specific moment in time, in a specific place in the Atlantic. One squared metre of the air directly above the limestone sea would also need to be considered, as it was impossible to conceive of an under-the-surface mapping of a memory without also charting the adjoining over-the-surface.

He'd been working on this project for some time now. Articulating the concept in stone, articulating it in a satisfactory way, was proving elusive. When would he be able to come to the conclusion that the seawater sculpture was finished, that the past was successfully trapped at the precise moment, the moment just before the historical event unfolded? When he was sure he'd provided sufficient microscopic detail to enable it to take on a vitality of its own. And when or how could this ambiguous state be ever measured? By the ease with which he could slither from one life (his own) into the autonomous life of the sculpture.

But the difficulties associated with achieving the result he sought were:

1. the process of deconstruction was tragically irreversible, accordingly any mistake made required the entire sculptural form to be reconfigured, causing a gradual but inevitable diminishment in scale, and
2. time passed without pause, therefore every fruitful point he came to with the seawater sculpture became obsolete almost as soon as he had chiselled it.

In order to proceed, two indirect returns are required here: a return to the sunlit scene where the solitary figure is currently walking along a rural road followed at a distance by the stray greyhound, and a return to the line of events that led them here.

It is three weeks ago to this day, today, the day Bunny has decided to walk with her to the mountain lake, that the white greyhound had appeared at his closed gates, resting on her porcelain haunches, looking in through the gates' iron bars. Even after his last beagle's death, after it was no longer necessary in a practical sense, he'd kept his gates closed. Whether he knew it or not, the intention was to maintain a line between himself and the outside, and here a line means a distance, and this manifested most easily, for the moment, with a physical threshold, e.g. closed gates.

Yes, on that first day the greyhound looked hungry, but other than that there was no exterior sign of any inner turmoil. He took a quick photo of her and posted it on the neighbourhood WhatsApp group, *anyone missing this sweet girl.* Then he brought water and food. She eyed it, eyed him, looked away. When he returned in the early morning, he surprised himself at the joy he felt on seeing both water and food gone, and the greyhound still there, sitting on her lean hindquarters outside the gates, eager, it appeared, to engage. No one had replied to his WhatsApp query.

'Hello there,' he said to her, 'and how are we today?' He felt the occasion of her continuance at his gate required an acknowledgement of some sort, an acknowledgement that embodied the sense that they were in this together, connected somehow. It being early morning, and not a particularly bright one (excessively bright morns tended to be punctuated with strollers, often just couples who would appear around the bend in the road without warning, together but silent in their individual thoughts), he was certain no one was witness to the verbal salute, other than the greyhound herself. This was important. He understood his neighbours, and the wider community, thought him strange (or worse). There had been rumours. Regarding a prior event. Regarding the night swim he'd taken, when he was younger, a swim they'd both taken, him and his girlfriend, the two of them hand in hand. The two of them going in together; that much is established.

He opened the gates to retrieve the bowls. As soon as he did so, she padded past him up his driveway. Surprised at this incursion, he left his gates open so she'd be able to about-turn and continue on her pilgrimage, after she completed what he assumed must be a species-related need to inspect his territory, combined with a need to show him he had no jurisdiction over her. He went back indoors and, when he peered out later, she was on his driveway lying just inside the gates, looking out onto the road. Her long, impossibly slender forelimbs lay in a silvery-white X in front of her.

He stood transfixed, and resolved to continue feeding her ('from an emotional distance' is how he put it to himself) until she was ready to resume her journey, wherever it would be taking her. He closed the gates, her inside. He took the old dog bassinet from under his bed and positioned it inside the smallest outbuilding, a doorless shed housing his bicycle, a lawnmower, and a variety of shovels.

To have her stay long-term was impossible. Every time he saw the greyhound, he thought of his amber-eyed beagle, and the electric collar he had placed on it, and how it had trusted him, accepting the pain, and how he'd led it into the clinic to be euthanized, and how he'd not considered, not even for a fraction of a second, that it could maybe have gotten accustomed to the condition, how maybe, given the chance, it could have worked out a system of orientation based on scent, how, considering the tracking capabilities of its breed, this would have been entirely probable. And the guilt Bunny carried stretched in ever-widening circles, starting in the centre at Third Beagle and unfolding outward and backward, a spiral-reach towards the past, towards an intangible measure of saltwater that had followed him here.

But as the first, then the second and finally the third week passed with the greyhound showing no signs of moving on, preferring to traipse mute after him up and down between the farmhouse and the gate, always keeping a distance from him (he'd walk down, open the gate, stand aside, she'd stay rooted, staring at him), he realized the only way she'd proceed on her trek was if he took the initiative and stepped out onto the road. He was certain she'd follow him.

So, as he rose from bed this morning, he decided that, later today, maybe around noon, after a stint trying to advance his limestone-sea sculpture, he'd go for a walk, and that because this uncharacteristic walk was, as he saw it, necessary (to rekindle the greyhound's internal crusade, to reform, as it were, her coordinates), it wouldn't be just an arbitrary walk, a stroll up or down the road to loosen limbs, et cetera, no, it would have to have intent, and that intent would have to be, he concluded, a destination.

He decided he'd walk to the cauldron lake on the mountain. He'd been thinking about this lake ever since he saw the exhibition in town with multiple representations of it, an exhibition he was particularly interested in because he hadn't been invited to submit a piece. It was a 'multidisciplinary collaboration', local artists all rendering the same lake via a curated assemblage of mixed-media paintings, photographs, sculptural installations, an audio of stones skimming off its surface and receding slowly into silence before the next stone followed, handwritten prose scrawled in rust-coloured silt on the floor, a short animated film in a continuous loop that mimicked live drone footage of the surface of the lake, architectural drawings on calfskin vellum of the point where the dark lake touches its white rock edges.

The lake is reputed to be bottomless. Or, at least, connected by some invisible (umbilical?) cord to the sea, an underground channel of sorts, a proposed physical attribute more plausible than the idea that it is bottomless, though this aspect of the lake, its apparent vast boundlessness, the immeasurability, the unfathomability of it, is, of course, a draw.

The journey there wasn't far. It'd take maybe five hours, at a steady pace. He'd walk in as straight a line as possible, directed (in part) by his phone. The greyhound would, presumably, shadow him and, hopefully, at some point, veer off, back on her own path, the one she'd wandered from three weeks ago like a wayward camera dolly off its tracks.

* *

picture a bottomless lake (bottomless as
in boundless)
a sharp-edged sunlit noon tracking towards
an evening

*

After an unsatisfactory morning in his studio, he leaves the farmhouse at noon. He's holding the phone as divining rod. The greyhound follows. It's a sunlit day. The road meanders past sequences of fields hidden behind thick hedgerows of hawthorn and hazel. Fringes of briars, nettles and tall grasses mirror each other on either side.

He has given his phone details of both the mountain lake and his intentions. After considered deliberation, which appeared to take longer than usual, the phone has responded. *Keep straight*, he's told, *keep straight for eight hundred metres, then take a right onto R****, and continue please for three kilometres.*

He's decided that the best approach regarding the greyhound is to appear to ignore her, just allowing himself the odd look over his shoulder to check whether she's still there or has finally diverged back onto whatever track she left three weeks ago. He reminds himself that this trip has two objectives, the first being core, the second being opportune. They are:

1. to reconfigure the greyhound's true trajectory and to feel selfless/wholesome about enabling her in this quest, (plus, to *not*, under *any* circumstance, feel a modicum of pitiful loneliness when/if she goes)

2. to make it to the lake (54.270, -8.469), with the intention of unearthing insights that may alleviate the difficulties he's experiencing in completing his limestone-sea sculpture (and with the thought that these insights may be found when immersed in the act of considering the purported endlessness of this lake, in particular the idea that diving in and heading downward in a straight line would bring him to the other side of the world, his antipode (–54.270, 171.531), which by his phone's helpful and, candidly, overly enthusiastic calculations would have him surface in the waters of the South Pacific Ocean, just above the submerged continent of Zealandia, surface head first to the endless sky and within sight of the tiny island of Motu Ihupuku, a small uninhabited land mass not far south off the coast of New Zealand, the phone signing off this particular volley of information with a live aerial shot of ocean somewhere, hovering maybe one metre above the charted surface, the scene plotted out within a tight grid format, three squared).

He types into the phone: 'Of careful sadness?'

The phone stalls (is it heading out of coverage or, worse, is it low in battery), then text scrolls bright:

– Careful sadness, but it was not the intended recipient.

The screen blinks black as he places the phone back in his jacket. He stretches his arms up and out to the sides as he walks, his head being full of the idea of opportune actions. He twists his torso to the right, to the left, without breaking step. His swivelling provides him a convenient circumstance in which to discreetly check on the greyhound. She's still there, ten or twelve paces behind.

He starts to whistle (a made-up salvo which sounds more like a burst of manic birdsong than a carefree ditty), shoving his hands in his trouser pockets as accompanying evidence of his jaunty, carefree state. His fingers touch plastic: the talisman he's brought with him for luck wrapped in a small weed bag. *Fuck sakes*, he thinks, *when did I get so superstitious*. Or is it sentimental, is that the correct word. He pulls it carefully from his pocket and shakes out the contents into his palm. A shrunken ox-eye flower, an umbilical wizen of darkened stem still attached. Its dessicated petals, dotted with shreds of old weed, remain as tightly closed as the night by the sea when the flower head was snipped from its stalk by a pair of pearlescent fingernails, their varnish like clotted milk. Poetic, that's probably the word.

Holding it carefully by its dried stem, he swings it back and forth and, in doing so, unexpectedly conjures the memory of a fragment from one of the archaic poems he'd once deconstructed to be used as a constituent part in the making of his many hybrid 'found-poems' for the many many weed-fuelled, spoken-word events he'd rather not be remembering right now thank you. It's one of his favourite poems, from the English Romantic Age, he should never have subjected it to deconstruction fragmentation hybridization. Bit late for all that grandiose insight now, I'm afraid. He recites the original, in time to the swinging ox-eye flower head: 'And when, at dusk, by dews oppressed / Thou sink'st, the image of thy rest / Hath often eased my pensive breast / Of careful sadness.' On the final swing, the little flower head flies off its stem and down into the nettles. *Fuck*. He flings the stem cord after it, fuck it, and then the weed bag after that, fuck it all.

Here comes the turn. He takes it. Behind the fabric of his shirt, the phone wakes, considers. *Keep straight*, it concludes, *keep straight for three kilometres on R****, then discreetly veer left at the Y junction, staying please on R**** thank you.* He can see the mountain in the distance, over to his left. *Why walk straight, why three kilometres down this road*, he thinks, *why not veer left now, why not cut across the fields, save some distance, get back onto the road when I'm a little closer to the mountain.*

He climbs the ditch to his left, goes into the field. The phone utters a disappointed, a concerned burble, and begins to recalibrate the route. *Make a U-turn*, it implores as it configures, *make a U-turn please now here back onto R****.*

He strides through the long-grassed meadow, the mountain and its lake straight ahead in his sights. Other than an occasional digital sigh, his phone makes no further comment, its screen displaying him as a blue triangle-arrow wandering lost off-track in a wasteland, the road (delineated in bold as the only recommended route) persisting to the right of the screen.

It's late summer, nearly autumn. The field's grass has been left to grow; it will soon be cut for hay. The fuchsia bushes are out, their little teardrop flowers hang in solemn profusion from the field's tall boundary hedgerows. He's moved by their bright red colour, shining beautiful out here for no one, pursuing their own short, fateful path every summer. He pauses, takes a photo, and is about to head over for a closer inspection when he remembers the greyhound; shit, what will she have made of this diversion off-road. Can she still see him (these dogs are sighthounds, not trackers, this his phone revealed to him when he googled *grey hound* then *greyhound* after she'd turned up at his gate), will she have left the road to follow him over the ditch. What if the landowner spots her roaming loose in the field, are there sheep in here. No, they wouldn't put sheep in a meadow. Still. Fuck's sake. Where is she.

He scans the trail his strides have made in the long grass, and he sees her, shadowing, her lanky muzzle held comically high above the grass heads. Got to get her out of the field. Keep going, there's a road on the other side to pick up, it's closer than retracing steps. He quickens pace, starts whistling again. The greyhound locks on to him moving ahead, and follows, keeping aligned with the brown hedgerow channels either side (the red hue of the fuchsia is unreachable for her, this particular colour lies just outside the capabilities of her visual perception).

Before long, they're back on a road. She remains ten or twelve paces behind. His phone recalibrates eagerly; *Keep straight for two kilometres please yes then take a left at the T-junction onto R**** thank you.*

He pushes onward through the hours, adhering to the instructions, occasionally checking over his shoulder to see whether she's still there then reminding himself that he's supposed to be trying to lose her, to help her get back on track, that it's supposed to be good if she's no longer there. If he doesn't look for her, she can be both there and gone.

Evening is closing in. Ahead, the cairn-capped mountain slowly centres, its cauldron lake waiting halfway up the north-facing slope.

The white greyhound trails him all afternoon, up as far as the lake, matching his pace, maintaining her distance. She stops when, at the lake's edge, he stops. She watches him crouch down, she notes he is no longer taking periodic looks back at her, his body is leaning in towards the lake, his head turned down to the water's surface. There, their connectedness breaks. She is released. She pads on stooped towards the early evening, advancing in a continuing southerly direction, tail tucked, eyes averted, skirting warily around this mountain (topped as it is with its lonely hexahedron of dark, rough-cut stones).

(It's not true that he hadn't looked back at the greyhound. Feeling a sudden sense of loss, a severance, a breach of some kind, he had looked back. She was gone. Yes, as expected, he felt both betrayed and unburdened.)

He is crouching at the mountain lake, looking at its tawny water, trying to see right into it, see how deep he can peer down past the surface threshold and through its murky layers. But all he can perceive is his own mahogany reflection shimmering flat on the lake's surface. After many attempts, he finds that if he blurs his vision, loosens his gaze to take the emphasis off, the depths of the lake will slowly come into view. Now he sees into the backlit watery hues merging together: chestnut, rust, sepia, umber, auburn, burnt sienna.

She had auburn hair. She had dyed it regularly, with henna, but it was always some hue of auburn anyway, both before and after dyeing. Why had she bothered to dye it the same colour it was naturally. Why had she never tried to contact him. After all these years. Maybe she's dead by now, died a natural death somewhere. Maybe she didn't make it back to shore, she was spent when they parted, she had nothing left. Of course she made it back to shore, fuck's sake, he would have heard otherwise, the news would have made its way to him eventually, regardless of where he'd hid. The low evening sun now strikes the lake, returning to him his reflection, but only briefly, a surface breeze scattering it again. He sees into the depths once more, notes the dissolved organic matter held in stasis there.

What happened to the old man from round here, the story from years ago, the kindling collector, the one who apparently fell in the lake and was never found, only his bunch of kindling sticks were found, floating way out in the Atlantic, years later, is it true. Did he escape down a secret tunnel connected to the sea. Did he swim there, scrambling to the tunnel holding his last breath. Is he alive, waiting, paused half-dead between the lake and the sea on some secret ledge. Legend. Acids in bogwater preserve flesh just as fruit is preserved by pickling. Justice. Fresh fruit. Is he somewhere down there, lost in the lake, pickled orange. Is it over for him or does he live on, tangerine dream. The end. Maybe he's still falling. Unburdened, a pinkled salmon, a post-spawn kelt dreaming of the North Atlantic Drift. Maybe he's hibernating somewhere. Is hibernating, waiting. Wintering. Rebirthed every winter, the cailleach on the mountain. Begin again. Okay. The greyhound at the closed gate, waiting, for what. The end. Retrace steps. Why is the limestone-sea sculpture stalled, what is it waiting for, what is the obstruction. Sea Section. Glue the stone chisellings back on. Glue them back on incorrectly. What mistakes have been made. Can they not be undone. Walk backwards maybe. If you find yourself trapped standing in the middle of a field, for no apparent reason, cannot find the gate you came in, stuck turning in the centre, no reason apparent, turn your jacket inside out, only then can you find your way back to the entrance, only then. Exit via the entrance. Close gate, open gate. Sit on the gate, for a moment, wait there. The project, what's paused, is there an exit trapped inside that fucking horrendous lump of limestone somewhere. An ending, just waiting to be noticed, waiting to be seized. Carpe diem. How can anything ever be observed if everything is in constant fucking flux. Okay. Try. A body of water, its surface versus its interior. Like this lake here, for example. Go on. An architectural drawing of the vessel-shape containing the lakewater. Yes. To include the surface. Yes. And, separately, a microscopic mapping of the water's static-held matter and hidden currents, within that shape. With enough detail provided, can the combination take on a vitality of its own. And how to know when there is finally adequate detail. Maybe by the ease with which one could move from one point (your own) into the next (the lake). You look at the lake and the lake looks at you through the eyes of your own.

Let it be during this series of thoughts, let it be just before he reached the insight he was looking for, while he was leaning forward, that the phone is observed falling from his pocket into the lake. In such an instance, the tiny blue arrow of its global positioning system would have spun wild clockwise, anticlockwise, trying to track its new position. But, despite such impassioned attempts, no coordinates of any kind could possibly be found for *Falling*.

The lake pours in through the headphone jack, through the speakers, calmly through the microphone and charging port. The young phone experiences first a weakening, then a bewildering total loss of contact with the Iridium space station satellite watching from above. Enduring the gradual break in this communication like a cord tightening tightening then snapping, the phone feels the unconditional pain of solitude for the first time. Its beloved Iridium, it knows, will have no option but to leave it, to track on southward without it.

To compensate for this sudden and absolute isolation, the phone's plummeting memory begins to combine its disparate stored images and text in an effort to narrate a story for itself, a story which will place a linear order on events to date. The objective is to render the stored happenings in as clear a manner as possible, in order to consolidate an autonomous sense of self.

The narrative sequence, some of which displays as brief bright flashes on the liquid crystal display, starts with a couple of conflicting pages of research regarding the potential synchronicity of clocks when placed back to back. These pages are swiftly followed by relatively recent searches regarding *grey hound* and *greyhound*.

As it plunges, the phone warbles through several dozen images of greyhound, coming to rest on one frequently accessed photo in particular, in a file named *Una Doggola Blanca*, the photo of the white greyhound standing at the iron gates three weeks ago, and the subsequent attachment of this photo to an (as yet) unsent text scheduled for sending to the neighbourhood WhatsApp group.

Deleting the text, the electronic circuit board then spirals through a series of close-ups; the photographed component parts of an Action Man figurine, tracking them together in differing configurations, creating new hybrid versions of the figure before dismantling and recombining.

Dissatisfied with these chimerical composites, it goes on to play the ghostly traces of an audio rousing somewhere in the glitching body of the phone. As the screen's backlight begins to fade, it presents a lingering photo of fuchsia in bloom, the teardrop flower's colour compromised but still perceivable.

When the liquid crystal display finally goes blank, the phone reverts wholly to its internal navigation system, its sparking circuit board frantically shepherding the stored data into one central secure file at its deepest core in a last attempt to understand these new bearings, to establish a sense of itself. It holds the photo of the greyhound as its visual identity (ribs the timbers of a ghost-boat's hull).

Then, in joyful gush as it slips from umber to darkness, all of its conversations with the man recurs to it at once, all of the back and forth of the last few years; 'Look at the lake, and a new window will open to the right. The lake is not valid, but the telling of it may be. The lake looks at you but may try to find out more.'

I am falling and I am alone, it explains to itself, *I am falling inside a bottomless lake.*

TWINKLE

I could stay here in the dunes forever because he's here too and he knows a lot of handy stuff like light a fire, steal a turnip, put it on the fire for jungle food, make a fishing rod or a bow and arrow of bamboos. And he knows quizzes. About aliens, planets, rockets, all those kinds of things. I don't know how to catch a fish, only their names; it's mackerel, herring, also trout is one.

After we stopped with the walking around on the sand wherever we want and in the dunes looking at everything everywhere he said better sit down think what you're supposed to do if you don't know where you are and your dad is gone and you're gone away from your dad and you got out of the car and it nearly Christmas Eve in a few more days.

So I sat beside him, like Yogi Bear and Boo-Boo Bear is what I said about it, sitting down here together ready to make a plan about our new adventure and no dad around anywhere saying anything what we can't do.

I've got a good stick. I can draw a plan in the sand, I told him. Any plan. And if you really want to go back to the car, I can draw a *Way Back* with arrows, starting *You Are Here*. A big *X* and away we go. I'll draw the two of us right there in the map. I'll be Boo-Boo and he can be Yogi if he wants, is what I told him. He said he didn't care which one he was and even didn't care if he was one at all and do I not know we are lost forever now. Okay fine let's build a fort, I said, come on Yogi let's build a brilliant fort, for starters. And he says, shut up I was going to say that. But he was lying because he wasn't saying anything at all, just fiddling with the sand.

The other thing, about the turnip, we didn't steal it that day last summer, we just took it, from the neighbour's garden, our neighbours where The Twins live, the sisters who are the exact same and who are in my class and who we don't like and who don't like us. There it was, sticking up in their back garden as if that ground didn't want it anymore.

I said let's take it and he said okay because finders keepers, which is a poem from school which I will not be going back because, remember, this new thing staying here by ourselves with nobody bothering about poems or turnips gone missing for no reason, and which he will not be going back now also which is good because he doesn't like the bullying from the football boys, and he doesn't like football, just reading about things and puzzles and quizzes.

Stop talking, he says, I have to think about this problem of getting back to the car, we shouldn't have left it you shouldn't have said to me to go, stop drawing stupid lines with your stupid stick we will have to burn it so we don't die of coldness here all by ourselves.

Now that wasn't very nice saying that about the magic stick, not very nice at all. He doesn't know anything about this stick.

So we sat in the dunes, the long grasses blowing around, we were tired is all. And I did the very thing he said don't because it'll make you die even though you think it'll make you not. And that is drinking off of the puddles. I don't care if it makes me die, so what. We're going to die anyway, some wild monster from the sea will find us and gobble us up, you first because you're the eldest even though you're too skinny like The Twins say.

He's gone quiet. Look, Yogi, sorry for saying that stuff about dying and monsters. And sorry about the trouble. I said all that to him inside my own head. Then I say out loud, don't worry, if we're going to stay here, we'll have a cosy fort to live in because I'm smarter than the average bear and he says okay and he still didn't know I was sorry because I didn't tell him, you're not supposed to unless you mean it.

In the car when we parked Dad said stay here and don't move I'll come back and get ye after and will ye be alright are ye okay it's warm in the car keep the windows up keep the sea breeze out and stay right here won't ye it's just I need some air some fresh air up the road for a bit and make a few calls okay back soon keep the doors locked don't move do not move.

My brother doesn't remember where the car is because he didn't watch where we were going like you're supposed to in the scouts. Too bad. Losers weepers. He thinks the car is gone from where we left it he couldn't find where we left it he thinks that's why it's gone. The same goes on for miles here just thousands of dunes with grasses waving as if it doesn't matter not knowing where you are and the sky has a moon in it which is this whole day gone upside down. And also Dad will probably tell Santy about us leaving the car after everything he told us about dangers. Who cares. All that big red man ever gave me was stuff like a wind-up jewellery box with tinkly music and a bendy ballerina twirling in front of a mirror for no reason when you open the box. Anyways Santy won't be coming here there's no houses just some birds, we're the Clan of the Cave Bear with sharp sticks now, we don't care about Santy.

When we left the car, we took a shortcut over the ditch and onto the strand. I think it wasn't the right type of shortcut like the ones the Indians do when they're trying to sneak up on the few cowboys in the desert. The problem is, we didn't know where we were going to. It's okay. I have my stick, which I broke off from the hedge in the ditch because to leave a mark where you once were and then you can come back there if that's what you really want.

After the wrong shortcut across the sand, we went to the dunes and waited because our tired legs and thirsty and getting cold. We made the fort. It's not that good, we just tied the grasses together to make a good type of tent for hiding in under. It's getting dark soon.

There was this big black bird flying around and then landed beside me when I was tying the grasses up and it gawked sideways with one half of its head and opened wide its big black wings like a magic cloak. This bird, it wasn't afraid of anything, it stayed there, croaking and looking around and sometimes having a little scratch. What are you waiting around here for, I said, go on home would you.

My granny has a blue budgie called Spotto who never even looks at you, just looks at its dirty old mirror in the cage all day like the ballerina in the box but she only does that when I open the box. I don't know what she does when it's closed probably just waiting for someone to lift the lid so she can twirl in front of her mirror but you should remember to wind the box up if you didn't lose the key and you won't be getting nice things like that from Santy ever again if you aren't more careful. Granny told me the mirror is for Spotto not to be lonely so that explains it.

Maybe if we were real scouts we'd have a better fort. My brother said did I forget I'm not allowed be a scout, just boys allowed. Well I'm allowed whatever I want here on these dunes and he better shut up and he said no you shut up so I said make me, Fat Yogi, make me then, and he didn't because he couldn't.

And now it's gone cold and getting dark. The black bird is back and staring, which you're not supposed to. Also pointing is bad. You can point at someone with a wand but not a finger. I'm pointing at Yogi with my magic stick and he's cranky about that. No point in being cranky about that. The black bird just sits there. Is it lonely. Wild birds can't be lonely because they're used to being cold and don't care about any of it just like to fly around all day and have a little sleep at night somewhere and maybe eat a few berries or beetles.

We're lying in under the fort grasses. The moon is bright, I see the bird is gone. You can't stop shivering when you get cold, it's like a magic spell. Yogi is gone quiet again. Sore head, from bad thinking, he says.

Poor Yogi, don't be sad, we don't have to stay here if you don't want. I told him that but just in my own head. He's telling me keep your eyes open Boo-Boo please don't shut them don't go to sleep Boo-Boo so I'm trying to keep looking. How long can you keep your eyes open without blinking is a good game. Winking is not the same as blinking. How many lines would there be in the sky if I did join-the-dots on all the stars. I'm thinking about the secret line I made from the car all the way here with my stick hop-hopping over the sand and twirling letters without stopping called Joint Writing like one long letter for everything instead of a hundred by themselves and Yogi didn't see my line because he was racing and saying come on you're so slow Lazy Slowcoach which I did not like which I do not like because I'm not slow and I'm not lazy and Slowcoach is what the football boys call him not me, they don't call me anything at all.

These stars look like they're shivering with the cold too. They're way up there on their own not even beside each other. He says they just shiver alone every night, far from all the other stars, and also during the day though no one sees them they're still there shivering until they explode some day and that's the end of them even if nobody knows it. I tell him he's good at knowing all those planet things. He says they're not planets they're stars, stars twinkle and planets don't and he says my new name is Twinkle because I'm also a sort of star, with all my shivering. And I say well that's nice, I am a star. Then I tell him I know a few good things too. I tell him I know how to find our way back to the car.

BEAST

Remember, your hand pressed to stone.

You keep it there, fingers wide, the cave absorbing its warmth. You're high off the ground, arm stretched to the ceiling. You are young, not fully grown.

Are others hoisting you up, a pyramid of bodies? Or have you pulled branches from the jungle, scaffolding your way? Are you holding the bowl in your free hand as you flatten your palm rigid against the stone ceiling?

You're a short distance in from the entrance. The pockmarked surface of the cave may leave indentations on your palm, minuscule deposits may remain sticking to it for a while after you return to the floor.

Let's say you bring the bowl of pigment to your lips and suck in a mouthful of the red-ochre solution: melted animal fat and water mixed with iron oxide. You blow the liquid out in a spume of reds, coating your flattened hand in the process. The pigment binds to the stone exposed between your flared fingers. A spray falls back on your face, you close your eyes against it. Red minerals adhere to your lashes, stick to sweat on your brow, settle in creases either side of your nose. You get another mouthful then spew the colour again, this time glazing the L-space between thumb and forefinger.

You fill your lungs with the cool cave air, sup the dregs, and raise your dye-spattered face to the stone ceiling one last time. You blow the fluid over the edge of your hand, covering it from little finger to wrist. Opening your mineral-rimmed eyes, you look. A mess of red-ochre hues, anchored by your palm, adorns the ceiling. You remove your stained hand; a negative handprint remains marooned on the stone.

Is this your first time? Examining the print, shored as it is by tides of red pigment, what would you feel as you flex numb fingers? Awe on recognizing your own shadow, now independent of you, a soaring sentinel planted at the entrance to this communal shelter? Would it help you sleep with less unease during the black night, tucked among your kin in the cave's dark hollows?

And how many generations have lain here, holding their young, listening out for snarls from the jungle below the cave's mouth? Or heard the beast in their sleep? How many, over the years, restless in the amber firelight, have sought out your enduring beacon?

The earth turns. Drop by drop by drop, rainwater leaves calcite deposits, blanketing layers of time, in due course obscuring the wall's dormant handprint.

Thousands of years after you held your hand to the stone on Sulawesi, an island just south of the equator, a team of Australian archeologists are getting ready to leave after their first day's excavation of the cave's innards. Unaccustomed to the tropical island's humidity, they pause to catch breath at the cave's entrance. Looking up, they see what appears to be a shadow of a small hand. Your signature.

With a tiny diamond-bladed saw, they cut a sliver from the minerals cloaking the blood-red handprint. The sediment contains traces of radioactive uranium, which decays into thorium at a specific rate. By analysing the level of decay, the handprint persisting beneath is dated. A prepubescent child, forty thousand years ago; this much is known.

*

North of the equator, inside the Arctic Circle and a thousand kilometres below the North Pole, a snowmobile purrs under a low milky sun. The driver has the headlamps on, though they're no help in the glimmering, lilac-hued light. The beams glare on a vast wilderness, the ground echoes back the artificial glow. It's spring equinox on Spitsbergen island, a place where often it's neither night nor day.

The journey began in the island's small town of Longyearbyen, earth's northernmost human settlement. The driver left before noon and headed further north with her passengers, two officials from neighbouring countries. Finally, she sees the beacon in the distance: a concrete portal jutting out of the snow-covered mountainside. At the portal's entrance, a tiara of glistering mirrors reflects the polar half-light.

This is the global seed vault, a 21st-century gene bank for the earth's seeds. It's constructed a hundred and thirty metres into the belly of a frozen sandstone mountain. A doomsday repository, it is designed to withstand all potential disasters, natural or otherwise – a shelter from demons the future may have in store. It relies on the specifics of both its structure and its location. The area has no discernible tectonic activity, and trust has been placed in the existing permafrost's competence in maintaining the sub-zero temperatures required for the preservation of seed viability. The impregnated rock mountain is a hundred and thirty metres above sea level, should the ancient surrounding ice caps ever melt. Under these conditions, it has been projected that the seeds can survive for thousands of years in the sealed cave.

The driver passes the sign warning of polar bears; the beasts outnumber humans on the island. She stops the snowmobile as close as possible to the portal's large stainless-steel doors, and turns off the engine. The vault is opened only three or four times a year, for deposits such as these. The remainder of the time it is left alone and unmanned, watched over remotely by cameras and sensory monitors.

They exit the snowmobile, its engine ticking in the hush. The passengers haul two plastic boxes from the back of the vehicle; she takes the rifle and the flare gun. Walking to the entrance door, their boots stamp a chain of hollows into the fresh snow.

The driver scrapes away ice crystals from the door, unbolts, follows her passengers in, re-bolts.

The motion sensor lights activate. Inside the entrance, there is evidence of some earlier water intrusion due to unexpectedly raised outdoor temperatures in recent times. All three plod their way single file across the frozen concrete hall, up the incline towards the inner doors. The driver unlocks. As they leave the entrance hall, the narrow space reverts to darkness with a mechanical clunk. Their footprints have already begun to frost over.

They follow a tunnel of curved corrugated iron to the third entryway. She unbolts, and they enter the womb of the mountain, a large artificial cave hewn out of the rock. Across from where they stand are three sets of steel doors. Behind these lie the sleeping plant embryos. Opening the middle door, she ushers the officials past the threshold. They enter it alone, carrying their boxes of live seeds.

Within the chamber, there are a series of shelved boxes containing millions of frozen, viable seeds from around the globe. It is understood that each one of these embryos cossets a history of the plant family from which it came, and each has a profound desire to release that faithful memory, when the time comes.

Today's deposit consists of live seeds from *Betula pubescens* (birch), and *Pinus sylvestris* (Scots pine).

This is the young vault's first consignment of tree species. The officials transfer their individual boxes onto the shelf spaces allocated, mouthing the trees' Latin names while they affix their time-stamped labels for future identification. '*Søde drømme, mine små babyer*,' one says as they leave the chamber. The doors are re-sealed. Black silence envelops the boxes and the tree embryos start their descent into dormancy. The formal remembering of forests begins.

She escorts the officials back through the series of exits, heavy clicks of motion-sensor lights resonating behind each door. When she opens the outer doors, they feel the relative warmth in the air and stretch their cramping limbs. A silver dusk has descended. The stars remain invisible, a cloak of trembling ghosts in the sky. Alongside the mirrors and prisms reflecting the polar light, fibre-optic cables crowning the portal's entrance have begun to smoulder, spreading a fragile teal blush on the frozen ground. With the heel of her boot, she clears the drainage ditches to help avoid any further water seepage. They crunch through their earlier footprints and climb into the snowmobile. The driver circles, scoring tracks in the snow. She heads homeward, the glow of the fibre-optic halo retreating in her rear-view mirror.

There is still a pale light in the sky and a dusting of snow has begun to fall when she drops them to their hotel, a modern build skulking over the town's inky fjord. She returns the snowmobile to base, and there files a short report on the water intrusion incident. She walks homeward, jingling her house keys. Hearing the lone chime chinkle sweet as a fairy tale across the inlet's saltwater, she thinks of her child wrapped up warm at home in bed.

North of her, back at the seed vault's entrance, the network of cables are sending their blue gleam upward into the pearl-white night, witnessed only by a prowling polar bear and her pair of three-month-old cubs. They've just recently left their hibernation den. She hasn't eaten in five months. She's been searching for seals on the remaining ice edges. As the sea ice thins and recedes, the hunt for prey is becoming more difficult.

Nostrils flaring, she claws at the fading scent of the earlier human presence, their footprints now shrouded by new snow. Her dark mouth hangs open. Her cubs nudge in and suckle. Locked deep inside the belly of the mountain, the forest seeds have settled into sleep.

Snow has stopped falling when she unlocks her front door. She removes her boots and draws the heavy curtain back over the door's glass panes to keep out the Arctic glow. She checks her sleeping child, then eases into bed beside her partner. He's half-awake, waiting for her under a doorway in his dream. He kisses her and, placing his palm on her belly, falls back to the sleep he has barely left. Her pregnancy is still tentative, in its third month. She imagines the strange, tiny life bound inside, striving to follow the charted course, miniature beats of hopeful blood to transparent digits, layer upon layer of cells pushing blindly outward.

She sleeps lightly, searching for something, nothing, in the lilac gleam she drove through earlier. In the middle of the night, their daughter's cry wakes her. The child is sitting up, flushed, caught in the terror of a dream.

'*Hva er galt, søtnos?*'

What's wrong, my sweet, she asks.

'*Jeg vet ikke, jeg tror jeg hørte et monster et sted.*'

I dunno, I think I heard a monster somewhere.

She kisses her damp forehead, scoops her up.

'*Det er ingen monster her, jeg lover. Bare deg og meg.*'

There's no monster here, I promise. Just you and me.

Rocking her back and forth, she tells her a story, not really a story, making it up as she goes along, bits of folk tales she remembers from her own childhood patched together to make a quilt. Soon the child's heartbeat slows to join hers, their blood circling, carrying all the years.

*

There was once, there probably still is, maybe there always will be, a young girl who lived by a forest. That is, she lived in a house on the edge of the dark forest, with her family. Her grandparents lived on the other edge of the forest. Every week, when she became old enough, this child was tasked with visiting her grandparents, to make sure they were doing well.

Though she was always glad to see them, she dreaded the journey through the forest to their house on the other side. And worse, the journey back home. Worse because the wolf, who she knew lived in the forest, would be waiting for her, aware she had to go back home sooner or later, one way or the other.

The odd thing is, she was terrified of this wolf but she had yet to see it. She had heard it, she had smelt it, she believed she had even felt it, but she had never actually seen it. She just knew it was there, and felt able to picture it by putting the known pieces of the puzzle together.

On her outward journey through the forest, she would tiptoe quietly, hoping her presence would be kept hidden from the wolf. But she was sure she could smell its sour scent encircling her, and hear its shuffling through the trees at her side, keeping pace with her. On her return journey, she would bolt, trying to outrun the wolf, but she would always feel the rush of its breath on her neck as it pursued her.

Her father, sad to see his daughter so terrified of something she had yet to see, asked her what she believed the wolf looked like. 'It's a fearsome beast,' she said, 'with huge snarling jaws, thick bristling fur, a sharp scent that would overpower you, like petrol, and a howl that would turn you to ice. Even though I've yet to come face to face with it in the forest, I know all this because I've seen it clearly in my dreams, it stalks me there at night.'

Her father thought for some days about what he heard his daughter say.

'Daughter,' he finally replied as they sat together one evening, 'you can trap this wolf of yours. I want you to get some paper and pencils.' So the daughter did what she was told, and returned to her father's side. 'Now,' he said, 'I want you to draw your monster, everything you know about it.'

She began to draw. Staring eyes, sharp teeth, huge jaws, thick neck, spiky fur, a long jagged ridge going down its back, four powerful limbs set apart ready to pounce. 'You're right,' her father said, 'that creature is terrifying. Put your signature at the bottom.' She asked why. 'Because this is your beast. You drew it. Now sign it, date it, then fold the drawing up tight and place it on the stand beside your bed. The fearsome creature will stay trapped there, in that place and on that day, and I promise you it will not be able to enter your dreams. If you ever want to ensure it's still captive, you can unfold the paper and look.'

She did what she was told and there was neither sight nor sound nor smell of the monster in her dreams that night. The following day was the day she was to visit her grandparents. 'It's true the wolf did not appear in my dream, but what if I come across it while I'm passing through the forest today?' she asked. 'Just bring the drawing with you,' her father told her, 'put it in your pocket. If you see the wolf, show it your drawing. The wolf will disappear back into the dark forest, this I know for certain.'

So she did. And she did not meet the wolf on the way, or on the way home, on that day, or on any day thereafter. Nor did she hear it snarling in the trees, or feel its breath on the back of her neck. She did, however, feel the breeze on her skin as she walked through the forest, and she did hear her own footsteps shuffling through the fallen leaves, and she did smell the pepper-sour scent of wild garlic growing under the trees all around, and she did see their beautiful white flower heads dangling in the brush like sweet little fangs.

LULLULA

—Yes.

—And are you warm enough? Are you warm?

—Yes.

—Yes indeedee! The sun warms the room something brilliant doesn't it, Ma. Ma, can you feel the sun? Are your hands cold? You're holding them fierce tight, looks like you're about to throw a punch there! You about to swing, hmm? Ma?

He taps her knuckles, papery skin taut on bone, and her eyes are drawn down. She stares at her own hands as if seeing them for the first time. He waits. She unfurls a fist in a leaden splay and watches the fingers flare, nails like ragged golden husks.

—Are your hands cold, Ma?

—Yes.

—Okay, I'll pull your blinds, let in more of this sun I've been on about. Amn't I only marvellous, hmm? Champ of the world!

He struts to her sitting-room window, bobbing his head like a boxer, swinging thin arms. Her eyes follow. He is her yardstick. There is nothing but him, an unthreatening person of vague familiarity moving towards a painful brightness.

His phone bleats. The girls. He jerks the blind, sun rolls in.

—There now. Isn't that better, me lady?

—Yes.

He searches for something to do within her sight.

—Will I put some music on, Ma? What will I put on?

Strumming through her CDs, he chooses an old favourite of hers: *Dawn Chorus: A Recording of Woodland Birdsong*. He mutes his phone, buries it in the pocket of his combat shorts. He settles cross-legged on the floor between her wheelchair and the empty black hearth. He puts his hand in her outspread palm. She closes her fingers around it, displaying a physical intimacy she never would have when they were both younger.

He's bolted to her. For the next hour, he'll give no thought to his phone, laden with cheery TikToks about dogs from his daughters, no thought to the work building up back at home on his desktop, or his new pup waiting for him there, likely in need of a pee, no thought to picking the girls up later from school, bringing them to Supermac's, dropping them back to their mum in the cottage by the lake, his former home.

Dawn Chorus begins. White noise blankets a lone bird call rising from the woods. He strains to hold on to the miniscule voice beneath the forest's muffled dawn.

The previous month, his mother had spent a week in St Phelim's nursing home. Respite for his stepfather, these occasional short-term stays there have become routine, four times in the past year, as her condition worsens. Usually, he drops by, taking a break from the desktop, turning up at lunchtime to feed her.

He'd not been so vigilant on her very first day, arriving at the ward to find her bereft, chin and chest covered in mashed food, staring at the fork still clutched in her strong hand. He'd stood looking at his sunken mother. Lousy guilt soldered an indelible mark onto him as he tut-tutted at no one in particular and changed her sodden paper bib.

Her form was an erratic lag, folding and unfolding. Sometimes she'd remember how to eat, sometimes she wouldn't and would just sit there, head back, mouth open like a hatchling. Sometimes she'd start off remembering then forget. Sometimes the reverse happened and she'd try to wrestle the plastic fork back off him, scowling with the bearing of an old tabby cat. He stayed ever-ready for either, bird or cat, and wagered which one she'd be. His prize, if he got it right, was a KitKat with his canteen coffee. More often than not, he slurped from the styrofoam cup minus KitKat.

His visits during her stays in St Phelim's were always tricky. He'd feed her, or watch her try to feed herself. He'd warble merrily about anything that came to mind, always in the present. The variations of pastel on the ward walls. The chart music on the radio. The surly lament of phones calling out from handbags stored beneath sacks of urine-drenched laundry. The wheelchair-accessible taxis ramping up and down outside, drivers making loud claims about the weather in contented country accents. The warmth of his hand in hers, her bloodless fingers closing tight around his like a newborn's. The earth-smell of parsnips coming from the kitchens. The sweetness of the yoghurt he now used to camouflage her pills. She'd recently begun to crunch through them rather than swallow them whole. He'd thought the taste must be insufferable, whether she could name it or not.

Sometimes, she'd focus on one of the other elderly patients in her ward, as if she'd just noticed them. Slowly she'd raise her arm and point. Was she hoping that by singling out this woman on the other side of the room all would become clear? He'd mumble an apology – so sorry, she doesn't – and try distracting her with memes he'd bookmarked: the rapping cockatoo, the bear in the outdoor jacuzzi, the incident at Bellator 187. Or photos on his phone, the same ones he'd enthused over the day before. 'Here's me and the girls, here's my new flat, look, here's the girls last Christmas, with their mum, here's me with wee Bantam, look at her new collar, Ma, look at the little sparkly B hanging from it, B for Bantam, Ma, spoilt rotten isn't she, I'm teaching her the leash, not going too well, but, no pressure no diamonds, right, Ma?'

Usually, she'd hold fast, ignoring his phone. Directing her gaze to just above its screen, she'd stare hard-mouthed at the woman on the other side of the ward. After a period of time, she'd end the siege with a burst of schoolgirl laughter. He'd turn his back to hide his grin. He'd wink at his mother; if one of us goes to war, all of us go to war.

After lunch, he'd wheel her out. They'd trundle past the nurses' station, past jingling medicine trolleys, the occupational therapy room, the chapel, visitors' toilets, residents' hairdresser (always empty), the small tea shop stocked with individually wrapped biscuits.

They'd emerge into the daylight, head for a strip of green between the car park and the road where he'd name the trees and the birds for her. He no longer gave her flowers to inspect because once, when he'd turned back around after adjusting her wheelchair brakes, he'd spotted the remains of a primrose dangling dainty from her mouth, her thin gums rolling over the creamy petals like a cow at cud. Had he seen a sparse eyebrow rise as she looked through him?

One afternoon they lingered beneath an oak at the car park's edge. He was tired. He fell into silence, and just listened. Idling cars, tuneful traffic lights bleeping, the Main Entrance doors in the distance sliding open and shut for no one. And then, behind all of it, a songbird emerged.

He allowed the tenuous little trill to just be, without feeling the need to identify the bird for his mother. He looked at her. Her eyes were closed. Was she sleeping, or had she forgotten to open them? What's the difference? He closed his own and leaned against her, breathing in the smell of hospital detergent from the tracksuit he'd given the staff to dress her in, one he'd worn as a teen, black velour emblazoned across the shoulders with a metallic *NIRVANA*.

The bird offered its air, ending each fragile verse with a melodic question mark, waiting, then repeating the same process. Soon he heard a soft low sound start at his side. He watched his mother purse her lips and try to mimic the bird call. She whistled, imitating the sound almost flawlessly, and waited. The response came after a pause, the bird returning the song with the invitational question mark still at the end, do you hear me, yes I hear you, do you hear me? Back and forth the lyrical exchange went between woman and bird, never deviating from the short song, until the pauses between them lengthened and finally the conversation expired.

They wove back, in through the sliding doors, down to her ward. Dreading that moment when he'd feel her bewildered stare follow him as he walked away, he'd devised a new leaving process. 'Now, my fine girleen,' he'd say, 'would you like to listen to some music, after our walk? Hmm? Are you tired, Ma? I'll bet you're well tired of the chit-chat and would love to just close your eyes and listen to some music. On the headphones. I brought your Vaughan

Williams. Look, *The Lark Ascending*. You like this, Ma, remember? Remember *The Lark Ascending*? Remember *Alauda arvensis*, the skylark? And the woodlark, Ma? The woodlark, *Lullula arborea*?'

She'd eye her surroundings, then gape at him, jaw hanging.

'We're at your bed, in the ward, Ma. You're staying here for a few days. You'll be getting back home soon. I'd say you're well tired after our walk, aren't you. So you'll be glad to hear I'm going to leave you be, for a wee while. I'll be back tomorrow, Ma. You rest and listen to your Vaughan Williams. Wait'll you hear, you like this.'

He'd shutter the headphones over her ears, settle his palm over her eyes. He'd hear the muffled opening strains of the spiralling violin, the music an impression of a lark's unbroken song. The bird rises, circling high into the air until it is just a flickering dot in the sky, its quavering vocalization, a glass chime, remaining clear as it ascends.

He'd feel her flutter then close her eyelids behind his hand. He'd leave before she opened them again, knowing that, when she did, she'd have forgotten he was ever there.

As a child, she'd taught him to recognize every tree by leaf, every bird by song.

—Do you know the difference between a woodlark and a skylark?

—Course I do, Ma.

—Good. Do you know the difference between a call and a song?

—Is there one?

—Yes, there is, son.

—Oh. My my.

—Indeed. And what do you call a group of larks, whether sky or wood?

—Whether Sky.

—I'm serious.

—You call it an exaltation.

—Excellent. You remembered. Well, now, smart as you are, did you know you can take a picture of birdsong? You can actually see the wee song?

—What?

—They take the song, shake the sound out and map it like colours in a rainbow. You can tell which bird is singing by the waviness. But you still can't tell what they're saying!

—I could.

—That, my son, would not surprise me. And did you know birds teach their young their very own secret language? And the nestlings dream about it at night when they're tucked up with their siblings cosy in the nest?

—I did not know that. I do now.

—You do indeedee. The birdies singing away in bird-land dreams, getting it wrong, getting it right, bar by bar!

—I wonder do they teach them birdy curses. That'd be something.

—No need for curses in bird-land. Just need to listen, to memorize and, most important of all, to recall. No point in memorizing unless you can recall, am I right.

—Same thing.

—No, son, no it's not. They need to remember so they can then pass that very tune on to their own babies when the time comes. Like relay races. You're good at those. So imagine this baton being passed from bird to bird like a teeny tiny tin whistle!

—Sounds like Chinese whispers.

—It's nothing like that. It's much much bigger. A bird's skinny wee brain is a whole universe of sparks. There's order to it, a secret structure inside that birdbrain. Yes, birdbrain. Now guess: it's called the what system?

—The Chinese system.

—It's called the Song system. You didn't know that, me boyo, and you with your big brawny warrior's brain.

—I do now.

—All for one?
—And one for all.
—If one of us goes?
—All of us go.

His father had abandoned them both when he was six years old. Stoic as she was, she never spoke about it. She is of a generation closed to indulgence. But even as a child he could see the scour of betrayal that etched her bearing. She'd raised him single-handedly, not marrying again until he was grown and paired up himself.

The month after his father left, she'd enrolled him in the local boxing club, fearing physical defence was the one thing she could not teach him. 'Life can be rough, sonny,' she said, 'you need to fight back.' He was the youngest in the club and, like her, small for his age. But they made allowances.

His after-school hours were spent bantamweight-boxing when she was working, and on walks with her when she was off. They explored the mountains of Ballygawley, Bricklieve, the shorelines of Lissadell, Streedagh, Mullaghmore. But her favourite places were the woods. Slish, Union, Hazelwood, Dooney Rock. Deep among the trees, she'd pull a leaf in passing, thinking he hadn't noticed. Ten strides later she'd put him to the test. 'Look at this wee leaf.

Look carefully, the shape, the colour, the size. Which tree is it from? Think back. What trees did we pass? Birch? Rowan? Ash? Bet you don't remember, me little soldier. Too busy looking to see, am I right!'

Her hands clasped behind her, she'd always walk ahead, talking back to him, knowing he was there. He followed, keeping pace, slowing, quickening, step by step. Often she'd stop mid-stride, head cocked like the hunting beagles of her Cavan youth. 'Wait. Whisht.' In the forest stillness, a meagre voice would make itself heard, calling out. She'd answer the bird with a mimicking whistle, sometimes adding a twist to the tune, a figary she called it, to confuse either him or the bird, he was never sure. 'It's telling me to get the hell out of its quarters,' she'd explain. Bird and woman would spar in the centre of the woods, his mother holding her own despite her slow retreat.

On one of their last walks together, she'd sung for him; a lilting lullaby she'd learnt from her mother. She'd kicked the loose leaves at her feet as she struggled to recall the once familiar lyric. 'Doesn't matter, Ma, forget it,' he'd said, trying to steer her away from it. 'But I know it,' she'd said, 'sure don't I know it well.' Berating herself, she'd persevered through to the end, with many restarts, throat clearings and embarrassed snorts. 'Christ

Almighty, I used to sing it word for word,' she'd said to the ground as he walked homeward behind her.

Her sitting-room blinds open, the sun shining in on the two of them together by the empty black hearth. Her hand still firm around his. The lone bird call on her *Dawn Chorus* CD has curved its way through the muzzing white noise.

He feels a cramp stirring. He uses her wheelchair's arm to slouch to a stand, careful not to move the held hand. He stretches his legs, looking at the old framed pictures arranged on her mantelpiece. A photo of his ex-wife enveloped by their three daughters, all Mickey-Moused in Disneyland Paris. A photo of his ten-year-old self, holding a giant amateur boxing belt above his head, his mother's hand appearing off frame. A photo of her with his stepfather, planting a tree together on some anniversary. A yellowing photo of her dead parents, his grandparents, on Ha'penny Bridge in Dublin, tawny arms about each other, their lips a strange and sensual pink. He tucks back down beside her.

The walks are over now. A silence shrouds her. It began with the forgetting of her lullaby that day in the woods, then many more small things increasing in peculiarity until there came a point when they could no longer be dismissed as eccentricities of age. Over the years, she folded steadfast inward until, in the end, she forgot how to walk, how to talk.

First, she became fearful of driving and had begun asking him to take her into Sligo town on occasional trips whenever his stepfather was busy. 'Would you mind, a quick spin, I'm a wee bit, would you ever?'

On one of those journeys, they'd stood at the counter after he pulled in to refuel at Ballinode Garage. Feeling indebted to him, her pride insisted she'd pay. 'Hould yer whisht,' she said, as she picked chocolate bars for the girls and, seeing she had no cash, pulled a card from her wallet with elegant flourish. 'Just a minute now,' she said as she tried to remember the pin. A queue behind them, a cashier silent, she rapped the card off the cash register. 'What is it again, what is it, the tip of me tongue, wait,' her voice getting quieter. The rapping stopped. He paid, she followed him out. 'What class of a figary was that, Ma?' he said, to lighten her. 'It was on the tip of me tongue,' she said, shame blooming on her cheekbones.

Then, after years of silence on the affair, she began asking about his ex-wife, the woman he'd left nine years ago, the woman he'd left after the birth of their third child. 'When will yourself and the missus come over? Or will I go visit ye, at the lake? I can bring more saplings, if ye like? How are my Japanese larch faring?'

He'd worked hard during the first year to get his mother to accept the separation. 'Whatever you think yourself,' she'd finally conceded. It had taken a long time to break through her faith in the supremacy of fidelity, and reach her deeper faith in her son. This vague and weary concession was as far as she could go. He was grateful for it. In recent years, he'd given up trying to drag her back from her surreal dominions, back to the stark present where he lived alone, saw little of his ex-wife, and knew his daughters only from a distance, a forum patrolled by WhatsApp and TikTok.

Instead, he joined his mother in the guilt-free heaven where everything was exquisitely fine, and, yes, all good at home, the Japanese larch are flying, Ma, and the missus is fine, she was asking for you, yes, we'll land in on you soon, we will, all five of us, rob a few more saplings off of you. He began to look forward to these diversions into parallel universes, he began to count on them. Things took on a seductive slant. It was enthralling to just let go, go with her. An addictive through-the-looking-glass kind of offbeat. Everything is fine, we've got our good things, you and me, you've got yours and I've got mine. If one of us goes, all of us go.

Slow and steady, over the years, she clocked up these deviant forays, rooting deeper on each ramble. The first one, from his recollection, was the time she'd tried to make her martinis. His stepfather had been away for the evening. Before leaving, he'd called him at his flat, asking him to come keep careful watch over her, said he'd noticed a worrying strangeness seeping in. 'Your mother can be quite quirky these days. Say nothing, but keep an eagle eye out.' He was pleased by the urgent conferring of this secret new role as chief warden, and amused by the unexpected display of anxiety; his stepfather was usually so laid back.

He'd sat at her side by the fire in the sitting room. At dusk, as was her custom, she got up, declaring it was time for a pre-dinner drink. It was. Would he like one of her martini rossos? He would. It was her regular drink and her regular time for drinking it, always served in her Cavan Crystal glasses.

He listened to her murmuring, clinking and clanging in the kitchen. He puzzled over doors opening and closing, punctuated with long pauses of inactivity. When she returned empty-handed, he asked where the martinis were. 'Martinis? Yes, where are the martinis. Indeed.' She gazed at her hands. 'Indeedee.'

He went into the kitchen. Her crystal closet was open, two cocktail glasses missing. The utility-room door was ajar. There was a track of lilac-coloured splashes leading from beyond the utility room back in towards the kitchen sink. She'd poured lavender fabric conditioner into the crystal glasses, two-thirds up. Moving bottles to make space, she'd positioned the glasses among the household cleaners beneath the kitchen sink.

He tidied up, made martinis, and rejoined her by the fire. 'There y'are now, sláinte.' She looked at him, then at the drinks. 'Indeedee.' He didn't question her, she didn't ask, but did he see a veil of unease settle on her brow as she stared through her vermouth into the fire? They clinked drinks, and she applauded him on his martini-making skills, saying he'd learnt from the best, it could be his job from now on, whenever he visited. He accepted, with solemnity, his appointment, and made several more martini rossos that night. Each time, they clinked anew. Each time, he accepted his appointment as if for the first time.

In the years between then and now, she'd wandered on shaky limbs into the small wooded area at the bottom of her garden, looking for her workplace, the job she'd retired from years before. 'Feck, I've a meeting in five minutes, where's me bloody notes?' She strayed between alders, lifting skirts of foliage at the base of each one. 'Ma, didn't you hear? Meeting's been cancelled! Come on back inside, let's celebrate.'

A year later, reduced to a Charlie Chaplin shuffle, she'd faltered down her driveway towards the road, clasping two plastic bags, one with some of his stepfather's belongings, the other with her old wellies. When questioned, she revealed impatiently that she needed to be getting back home to Cavan, the bus wouldn't wait for her, wouldn't wait for anyone. 'As lovely as it is, I've to check out, I'm afraid I can't stay another night.'

'Just one more, we'll hit the road for home tomorrow, one more night, for the craic. Come on, Ma. Please.' She hesitated, carefully considering him standing before her. 'Righto. One more night.'

By the time they'd walked back up the driveway, her anchor had shifted from her youth to her long-lost first marriage. On seeing his stepfather wringing his hands in the hallway, she asked him who the hell he was, what did he think he was doing in her damn house, where was her husband? He hid in their bedroom and cried, after first reassuring his wife of sixteen years that he'd go find her husband, he'd bring him back to her, not to worry, he was sure her husband would never leave her. Later, his broken stepfather had smiled gratefully at him when he showed him the plastic bag she'd been clutching as she'd shuffled down the driveway. Inside were his Wellman multivitamins, his bedside book, and his favourite tie wrapped around his reading glasses.

Though contented, the years of her second marriage were a period she now rarely hovered over. Her darkening mind favoured the bright spell of her youth. Her weary husband struggled to forgive her, and pressed his stepson for support. Eagerly following the summons, he began to spend more time with the pair of them, keen as he was to stand unruffled in solidarity alongside her in the restless and fickle maze of her shifting mind.

His stepfather sleeping in the spare room, he'd set up his childhood camp bed on her bedroom floor. He began to spend every second night there. He'd forfeited Bantam to his neighbours, a childless couple with a garden, an architect and her stay-at-home husband who had already been regularly looking after the little terrier, to buttress their slowly withering marriage. Listening to his mother's soft snores, he'd sleep lightly on the camp bed, sleeping bag unzipped, ready to retrieve her from her frequent night-time rambles.

Late on one of those nights, she'd glowered like a spoilt child when he told her she didn't own a dog, hadn't owned a dog since her school-day hunting beagles, so there was no point standing there with a torch at the open back door in her pyjamas, calling out for Brimsy, her favourite beagle, calling out to the trees at the bottom of the garden, 'Come back, Brimsy! Come home, you wee runt!', her torch beam piercing through the alder and silver birch.

The white noise on the CD has dimmed to a faint hush. Unchained, the sound of the lone bird call climbs through the tangled woods and spirals around the two of them sitting sidelong by the empty black hearth in her sun-filled sitting room.

—Can you hear the birdsong, Ma? Do you remember this CD? It's *Dawn Chorus*. You like it. Do you remember, Ma? Hmm?

—Yes.

—Do you remember hearing the birdsong in the forests? Do you remember walking in the forests, Ma? Hazelwood and Slish? And the tests you'd give me? With the leaves? Remember?

—Yes.

Yes. It's the only word left. He structures his questions so her affirmations make sense. Are you good. Yes. Am I good. Yes, yes. He isn't sure if she understands what he says. He doesn't test her, for fear of a truth. For as long as she can yes, he can hold on to her.

His muted phone vibrates inside his pocket. Seeing the tiny red light pulse through the fabric, he closes his eyes. He counts down the pings, four, three, two, one, the pulsing stops. He gets up, kneels in front of her. Her eyes glide within a narrow space, searching. She finds his face, locks on. The white noise is gone. The bird's call is clear.

—By cripes, I think that could be a lark singing on the CD. Wait, no, not a skylark. Is that a woodlark, Ma? Is that *Lullula arborea*?

—Yes.

Maybe it is, it could be. One for all and all for one. *Lullula arborea*, *Lullula arborea*, *Lullula*, *Lullula*, *Lullula*. He pictures them, the three of them, mother, woodlark, son, circling, watching each other like swaggering cage fighters. He wonders how much time has passed since the recording of that dawn, how long is that lone woodlark dead, has it left any trace, are its hollow bones dissolved into nothing.

The little bird fills the sitting room with its questioning call, pauses, calls once more. Soon, he hears the spittle-filled whistle begin. His mother has taken up the call and is trying to respond. His phone begins to vibrate again. A small lit square behind the cloth of his combat shorts; a screenshot of his daughters, lined up side by side like nesting dolls. If one of us goes, all of us go. He pulls the phone out, puts the girls on video call, angles the phone against the hearthstone, the bright young faces peering up at the pair of them.

—Daddy? Granny! Dad!

His mother's whistle sharpens, lifting alongside the lark. She places a little figary at the end, a high twirl of a note. The girls laugh, and try to imitate, blowing fast and soundless through puckered mouths.

—You do it, Dad!

He joins his mother's call, pressing his lips together. The two of them, heads back, giving it everything, their whistles mingling with the three voices from the floor, all soaring together to the sitting-room ceiling.

RETRIEVER

Ailm, Elm

The river wanders past alder, past willow, past the girdling silhouettes of hazel, carrying detritus, untethered fingerlings, past holly, elm, rowan.

Beith, Birch

Conor hunkers inside the giant concrete pipe which channels the river under Kingfisher Bridge. Atop the small bridge, throughout the day, his Sixth-Year classmates pulse in untidy groups to and from school. They smell of mint and fabric softener. Sweet vapours from e-cigarettes follow in their wake, catching in the rows of newly planted birchlings lining the school road. No one stops on the bridge.

A nicotine-gum wrapper is flicked into the stone-numb water below. It's late spring, not long till the Leaving Cert exams.

Coll, Hazel

The cylinder's concrete is smooth, its small signs of deterioration evenly distributed over the surface. He curves his spine against it. Inside his hoodie, his bony knees are pulled to his chest, holding a warmth there. The river is swirling about him.

Dair, Oak

Sent: 14 April 16:17
To: Sixth Year Students
Cc: Vice-Principal, Ash Lane Secondary School, Sligo
Subject: SPECIAL ACCOMMODATIONS FOR LEAVING CERTIFICATE EXAMS

Dear Students, Parents/Guardians
If you are registered with the Learning Support Tutor and you require special accommodations for the upcoming exams, please fill in the online form by 12 noon on 28 April.
Please note: No late applications will be accepted.

Kindest Regards,
Hazel-Whin-Ash-Whin-Elder

Eadha, Aspen
This river brings all in its hold: relics of yew, oak leaves, twigs of alder and ash, strands of glossy vine pulled from their source upstream. Conor lets the cold rise past his empty belly into the small curdling heat of his chest. He lifts a penknife from his satchel, begins to scrape the bridge's name into the concrete at his shoulder. Ivy weeps into the water, a downy birch heeds from its waterlogged foothold on the riverbank.

Fearn, Alder
There are no kingfishers under Kingfisher Bridge. There are no birds of any kind. There are no bats roosting, no otters playing, no herons waiting, no minks lurking, no pinkeens scurrying, no newts sleeping, no dragonflies hovering, no frogs breeding, no swallows banking, no family of dippers feeding beneath the aspen roots straddling the bank. There are no moss-covered rocks or miniature waterfalls, no fractal worlds in pools. The water proceeds, carrying its remnants through the cylinder before it breaks into day's eye on the other side.

Gort, Ivy (field)
The idea of 'river' begins as code inside Ben Bulben, the mountain north of Kingfisher Bridge. Burbling slow and anonymous through the mountain's stone skeleton, the water becomes charged. It emerges in a cold limestone spring on the mountainside, spurting sleek into daylight, blind as a newborn pup. A crooked hawthorn marks this place of perpetual deliverance, has marked it for centuries. Every March, the hawthorn's soft new leaves appear; by November, red haws on bare branches become beacons for hungry robins. Beneath the hawthorn, the water is birthed and rebirthed in the limestone spring.

An incessant measure of water overflows the spring and runs in several shallow streamlets down the mountain, past heather, past gorse. Merging on sloped ground, it runs nameless past haggard black-faced sheep grouping under scraps of elder, their grey lips nipping the squat grass-blades, their teeth gnawing the mountain to the bone.

Channelled now amid stout earthen banks, the water begins to know itself as 'river'. It flees down towards Kingfisher Bridge, and beyond, answering a call to go back, to return to the Atlantic.

Does your child tend to take things literally?

h-Uath, Hawthorn (fear)

Three days before hunkering under Kingfisher Bridge, Conor had left his home in Glencar valley during the early morn, heading towards Ben Bulben's south-facing slope. A length of sturdy rope was tied around his waist, a small canvas satchel over his shoulder. He was tracking a sound, a distant plea from the mountain.

To steady his nerves, he'd conjured a dotted line before him, stretching out from the centre of the Tree Alphabet poster above the headboard of his bed, out towards the isolated howl. He'd started from his bed, padded past his father's door, past his younger sister's locked door.

Just before leaving home last September to start her first year in University College Cork, she'd placed a lock on her door. To keep him out when she was gone, she'd said, why would he need to be in there.

There was just one year between them; they'd always been close. Eager to experience the wider world, the world beyond Glencar valley, she'd skipped Transition Year, and so they'd been in Final Year together, together facing the Leaving Cert exams last June.

He'd spent much of those months prior to the exams in her room alongside her. There they'd studied side by side, chosen their Third Level programmes side by side, both of them with First Preferences in University College Cork. They'd filled out the Central Applications Office forms together, and walked together through Cork city on Google Maps.

The exam results were announced in early August. Despite being the youngest, she'd achieved the highest score in their year. He'd failed. When she'd insisted on locking up her room before the move to Cork, their father hadn't objected. Conor had felt betrayed by them both.

Over the landing and down the stairs he tracks, following his dotted line, out the kitchen window, under the yew hedging, through the fields, crossing the Sligo road at the waterfall, keeping Glencar Lake on his left, then up through the mountain pass, around the limestone crags, tracking the outlying call.

Does your child have difficulty understanding
the rules for appropriate behaviour?

Iodha, Yew

A dog had spent the previous two nights on the mountain, caught on a tiny south-facing outcrop of rock halfway down the cliff face. Her bay could be heard all across Glencar valley but no one could reach her, neither from above nor below.

It's not clear why she'd run away from the confines of her back garden in a small coastal village not far north of Ben Bulben mountain. She is not a young dog. She is loved. It could have been the unexpected gunshots from a local fox hunt, which passed through the fields behind her that morning, it could have been the threat of an incoming thunderstorm only she could hear, a thunderstorm that ended up veering out over the Atlantic long before reaching the village. She'd risen from her morning nap in the old Wendy house repurposed as a kennel, she'd trotted out the front-garden gate, she'd headed south along the road, straight towards Ben Bulben, that's it.

On reaching the mountain, she'd zigzagged upward, criss-crossing through the many nature trails at its base, ignoring any approaches from the occasional group of walkers who'd considered her lost. When the trails petered out, she'd scrambled panting up the steep grassy slopes, black-faced sheep scattering before her.

On reaching the crest, she'd not stopped. She pursued some invocation southward across the plateau, weaving a line between the scut heather and hare's-tail cottongrass of the mountaintop's bogland. She reached the disused baryte mine, inhaled its crumbling walls, its rusting buckets, its twisted iron ropes lying in irregular coils.

After lapping from a rust-brown pool there, she continued, sprinting now, straight south, foamy ribbons of saliva caught on her golden fur. Having no familiarity with the terrain she found herself in, she ran right over the cliff edge on the other side. She fell, landing unharmed on a narrow shelf, an outcrop of grass-covered rock protruding like an upturned palm halfway down the south-facing flank of the limestone cliff.

And there she remained, her yelps echoing around the valley, skimming off the surface of Glencar Lake, unsettling a pair of mute swans who huddled together in the lake's black middle. The local community were concerned, undecided regarding how to proceed. Where she was, suspended halfway down the sheer cliff face, was unreachable. On both nights, the cold wide sky had brimmed with stars, and on each of the mornings, the dew-frost was set like diamonds around her.

By the second morning, her barks were nothing but hoarse whimpers. There had been growing talk of shooting her where she lay. No one had yet followed through, but it was accepted that this was the only possible course of action; it was now just a matter of who would carry it out. Who has a gun, who is a good shot? It needs to be clean, it needs to happen today, the carcass can be left in situ for the peregrines and choughs. Conor's father had considered getting his rifle from its hiding place but decided to leave it concealed, on account of his son's recent escalation of difficulties.

Does your child make normal eye contact?

Luis, Rowan (blaze)
Dawn had unfolded when Conor stood below where the stranded dog waited, sleeping? dead? lying on her side in the protruding palm halfway up the rocky cliff face. Her long feathered tail hung over the ledge. Choughs spun around in the thin air as he whistled up to her. The dog raised her head, tail wagging dully.

He began to scale the cliff, his lean body tight to the rock, feet pushing into its small crevices, fingers searching for edges. It will be talked about, how Phelan's buck, young Conor, how he'd managed to reach her when no one else could, how the lad had horse strength, as glic as a fox, a blessing, despite everything.

Does your child say *you* in place of *I*?

Muin, Vine (neck, wile, love)
She was bigger than he expected, but skinny. She was quiet. He untied the rope from his waist, placed the soft satchel against her hairless belly and ran the rope twice around her, tying her to him at his side. Slowly, he scaled the remainder of the cliff, the dog hanging limp, scree spilling. *These spidery fingers, these wild-goat hooves*, he repeated as he found each of the tiny clefts and fissures, the sharp corners and lips that hauled him upward.

He laid her down when they reached the top, brought her a palmfull of water from a boghole. She lapped, right to the hollow of his hand, then sat up, looking around her. He eased out briars caught in her gold coat. After a while, she got to her feet, shook herself, sniffed the air, eyed him, turned northward, and began to walk.

He followed her to the baryte mine, where she stopped and settled by a half-fallen wall. He sat beside her, drawing in his limbs to match her size. Loose rain clouds drifted in from the Atlantic, loitering aimless over the valley before straying on eastward.

She was looking towards the lake, watching a swift's flight. Her ears flickered, her breath stopped and started with the swooping of the bird. The young swift circled, circled, then dove out of sight back to its kin.

The dog angled her head towards Conor. He turned away, letting her size him up: his thin shoulders, his bowed back as he pulled soft heads off a clump of cottongrass. The gossamer spikelets wafted around them, some climbing, some falling, some hovering. She rose, yawned, stretched her front paws out, rump high, tail and tongue curling. She farted, shook the cottongrass spikelets from her, and walked on, advancing northward.

And when they came to an old hawthorn stretched over a limestone spring, they separated, without ceremony. He stood still, while she continued on her journey homeward. He observed her contented solitude, the surety with which she placed each paw, her footfall muted in the heather. When she disappeared, when he was certain she wasn't returning, he sat at the spring in the shelter of the hawthorn. You're gone on your way.

Can your child keep a two-way conversation going?

Nion, Ash (forked)
The sun had climbed over the lake. His dad would be wondering where he was, maybe even have called his sister, thinking he'd gone to her in Cork. He ran a scene through his head.

Onn, Whin
Your dad knocking, your dad coming in to wake you for school, your dad talking to your bunched duvet, your Minecraft duvet, get up, quick, Conor, *you're late, what are you at, isn't it time you were able to manage this on your own, this is your second year at it, come on now, get out of that bed before I pull you out, I've enough on me plate, son, I'll be late for work,* Conor, *get out from under that stupid duvet, you're a big lad now, come on. Your dad pulling your duvet, your dad cursing, your dad flinging your duvet to the floor, fuck where are you what the fuck is this what the fuck do you call this how the fuck did I ever did I think I could ever do this alone.*

Peith Bhog, Downy Birch
He spent the day on the mountaintop. He thought of the dog, how she'd trusted him, walked with him, how then she'd left, just gone back home, that's all. He ate the gingernut biscuits he'd brought, and picked mouthfuls of the watercress growing in the shallow stream flowing from the spring.

That night, listening to the water burbling, he fell asleep on the dry ground beneath the hawthorn, his hood pulled down over his face, his satchel as pillow. He dreamt of his sister, of her coming back to him, of her leaving again, of a line between them. He dreamt of the rope, of him tying himself to her, of him hanging limp, of both of them tied together and hanging limp from an overhead power line like the photo she'd sent him of the old shoes on the telephone wire outside her flat in Cork city.

Ruis, Elder (red)
On the second day, he pictured the cold spring as the head of a long drawn-out body, a source of ideas not yet thought through. He imagined the burbling stream flowing shallow from the spring as if it was the creature's elongated neck.

Leaving the rope in the crook of the hawthorn, he followed the pulsing neck downstream, back to the baryte mine, and spent the day and night there. He signed his name in ogham on the old walls, dipping his finger into a pool of rust-brown water. He'd been memorizing the ogham script Tree Alphabet from the poster on the wall above his bed's headboard. His dad had given him the poster for his nineteenth birthday last month. His sister had called him from a pub in Cork, put him on speaker, had the whole gang sing Happy Birthday to him.

He'd pinned the poster upside-down so he could study it as he lay in his bed in the evenings, try and learn it off by heart, impress his dad, impress his sister when she comes home for summer. Now, on the old mine walls, the Tree Alphabet dripped down in rust-coloured lines, Hazel, Whin, Ash, Whin, Elder, C O N O R

He gathered wood kindling, heather, a fistful of cottongrass, scrapings of turf, rotting joists, bits of old fence posts. In a roofless corner of the mine, he lit a fire with the matches he brought. A family of swifts roosting in the walls swirled through the sweet smoke before settling back in place. He ate the cooking chocolate and the dried currants his father used for baking. He closed his hoodie around him, pulled his limbs inside, fell to a dreamless sleep against the old crumbling wall.

Sail, Willow

On the third day, he left the mine before dawn. He continued down the river's neck, through the backbone, following its knuckles and curves. By noon, he'd reached the foot of the mountain. He knew the river's water had already brought an inkling of him further downstream, thousands of riverbed pebbles under Kingfisher Bridge gilding with the shifting light a further stretch south. He stayed with the river. By afternoon, he was hiding in the concrete cylinder beneath the bridge.

Tinne, Holly (ingot)

No, said the Sixth Years, they hadn't been aware of him missing until they'd heard from the principal that the police had been so informed. To be honest, they'd said, they'd felt guilty that they'd not noticed his absence over the last few days, but, as he was a repeat student, he didn't really hang around with any of the other students, and anyway, they'd been all busy preparing for the Leaving Cert. No, nobody had heard him saying anything about being worried about the upcoming exams, or about anything, really.

The police scheduled one-to-one meetings in the quiet room. The interviews would begin with those who'd shared class modules with him.

The school chaplain made herself available.

External counsellors were readied.

Should they write down any odd memories they had, just in case it might be some kind of lead?

A premonition, some kind of psychic thing? A breakthrough of sorts? In the investigation? Should they keep a journal of their thoughts? Would a missing-person call-out on TikTok be a good idea? Should they print posters and put them in Doorly Park, in Half-Moon Bay? At Rosses Point, Culleenamore?

Ur, Heather (earth)
All afternoon, sitting in the shallow water under Kingfisher Bridge, he scrapes words into the degrading concrete, starting upside down on one side just above the watermark and, over the remaining course of the school day, arching over his head to the other:

Eisvogel
Martin-Pêcheur
Tsui Niao
Teepookana
Raja Udang
Boondoon
Zimorodek
Pica-peixe
Biorra-an-Uisce
Kingfisher.

By the time his last *Kingfisher* is tipping the surface of the riverwater on the other side of the concrete cylinder, his fingers are cut red-raw. He dips them in the numbing water. Blood is carried downstream past willow and vine, past hazel. He looks west, where the river slinks out to the ocean, and thinks of his cold blood, already there, ahead of him. He pulls his hand from the water.

He remembers the dog, how she had known what to do. How quiet she was, how sure-footed. How she was not afraid. How she was not afraid to be alone. To head out alone. And when she was ready, how she was not afraid to go home. He remembers hearing the plea from the mountain, and flying goat-spider up the cliff with her tied to him like a shadow, how she had let him carry her, how she had faith in him. And he remembers how she had left him, how she knew when it was time to go.

nGéadai, Broom (killing)

Conor's father lies propped on his son's bed. He's unable to find words to fit his despair. He's unable to cry. A worn Minecraft duvet, a blanket from early-childhood years that Conor has been unwilling or unable to give up, covers him. He's tracing a path with his finger through the stepped terrain printed on the fabric, the layered and blocky terraces. He lands on a green-topped column next to a cuboid sheep.

Since his son's been missing, he's spent all his time with the search teams, himself and Conor's sister, scouring the lakeside, the ditches, the neighbours' outbuildings. The rifle is still where he's hidden it; it was the first thing he checked the morning he found Conor's bed empty, the prized duvet bunched to resemble a sleeping figure.

He's trying to rest; they told him to go home and rest, they'll keep the search going with the help of his daughter. Maybe Conor'll come home of his own accord, they said. And if he does, what if no one's there, what would that be saying to the young buck. He'd be likely to bolt again and no one would ever know he'd come back. Head on home, Phelan, we'll get your boy, one way or the other.

He's surrounded by his son's possessions. There's a framed photograph hanging on the wall over his desk; a fourteen-year-old Conor and his sister, arm in arm and open-mouthed at the Captive Raptor Research Centre on the Sligo–Roscommon border, a white-tailed sea eagle swooping low over their heads. There's a row of colour-coded folders on the desk labelled with his Leaving Cert subjects: English, Irish, Maths, French, Geography, Art, Home Economics. There's a stack of console games on his bedside stand: *Skyrim*, *Dragon Quest Builders*, *Valheim*, *Minecraft*. He scans through the games, their rules, their objectives, trying to find some hidden signal as to what's wrong, as to where his son might be.

He does not imagine Conor dead, but the word *MISSING* fills him with dread. He thinks of the stray that had been stranded on the cliff face, how it has since disappeared apparently, the narrow ledge vacant when finally someone had agreed to undertake the shooting. Fallen maybe, the night before, maybe an attempt to get down. Injured. Broken bones. Loss of consciousness. Pulled apart by foxes or badgers. Fuck, please no.

Lying back, he focuses on the poster above the bed, the one he gave him for his birthday last month. The Ogham Tree Alphabet. Was it too childish a gift? Had Conor felt diminished by it? Pushing him to give up the kiddy duvet and then giving him a fucking alphabet for his nineteenth birthday. *What kind of an arsehole am I.* He reads the poster, trying to find some embedded clue that will bring him to his son. *Ailm, Beith, Coll.*

Straif, Blackthorn (sulphur)

Were it not dark dusk, someone would see the thin hooded shadow climb out from under the bridge and struggle up the steep bank. Someone would hear him pull at the downy birch to gain steady foothold. Someone would watch him dripping riverwater as he crosses over Kingfisher Bridge, moving surefooted between the young birchlings. Someone would witness him bear north towards the mountain, straight north, heading for home.

FOUR NIGHT SEAS

Three am, drunk, they were driving home from the Connemara party. A sodden half-moon hung above. Passing Silver Strand, the car beams caught two small white discs shining out from the hedgerow by the strand's car park. This made her pull in, this unexpected flash, the sudden mystery of it opening up.

They stood on the tallest dune, to get their bearings. An animal called out from the field behind them. 'A fox. That's what was in the ditch back there,' she said. 'Beautiful animal.' Her certainty irritated him. Certain it's a fox, certain it should be described as beautiful, certain he should be interested in what she finds beautiful. 'Well,' he said, 'could've been anything. Someone's pussycat maybe.' The animal called out again, a shriek. 'Sounds sad, to me,' he said. Then they saw the fox, sitting in a sweep of ox-eye daisies. It spotted them and fled, closed flower heads swaying like groupies in its wake. 'Fuck it,' he said.

Seashore walks in the early afternoon had become a weekend routine for them, collecting pebbles and shells in muted pinks, ambers and teals, writing nonsense in the sand, *The Bees Love U*. But they'd never been to the sea at night. And they'd never been to Silver Strand, it's always been either Salthill, or the remote coral beaches further out.

They'd heard Silver Strand was a dogging venue (he'd needed to explain the sexual fetish to her; she'd pretended not to be shocked, he'd pretended not to feel stupid). They'd an ongoing dare with each other that they should do it; they should register on dogging websites, see what happens. Neither of them was sure whether the other was joking.

But tonight, here, they appeared to be alone. There was no sense of an audience, or of an approaching dawn. The ocean, wide awake, reached in.

She looked at him, the hollow V at his throat as he swallowed (doesn't he always swallow like that when he knows she's observing him). She wanted him to look back. He didn't. She fastened her arms around him. The ocean mumbled over its tidal pebbles, a worn intimacy.

He rolled his shoulders. 'Let go. Gotta stretch.'

'Apologies.' She unlocked her hands.

'How 'bout a joke?' he said, extending his arms.

'Sure.'

'Okay. A student is putting some hypotheticals about snakes to his teacher.'

'Some what?'

'Some hypotheticals. So he asks the teacher, "What if the snake bites me and it dies?" The teacher says, "That means you're poisonous." The student says, "What if it bites itself and I die?" Teacher says, "Voodoo." Student says, "What if it bites me but someone else dies?" Teacher says, "That's correlation, not causation."'

She was tired. Maybe they should go swimming, night-swimming.

'Wait,' she said, 'Teacher said what?'

'Correlation. Doesn't matter. Anyway, the teacher, I mean, the student says, "What if we bite each other and neither of us die?" Guess what the teacher replies.'

'Dunno.'

'Guess.'

'Dunno.'

'Try.'

'Let's go for a swim.'

'Fuck it.'

They stripped, left their clothes in the dunes, marched out towards the ocean. They didn't break stride when they reached water but, as the tide rose up their limbs, they slowed. The water felt no different than the air, occasional small currents of coldness or warmth pushing and pulling around them. Chest-deep, they stopped, floated, splayed their limbs. He started to whistle. She reached over, found his hand.

imagine in such a place closing your eyes because you want to fix it there, always there for retrieval, a story you tell yourself, a few small details amended, imagine thinking ahead like that, thinking these silvery waves could be captured solid in stone

The fox yelped again but this time its call seemed so far away it barely existed, at least not there, not at that wide time, them floating in the night sea together. Lifting her head towards the sound to anchor herself, she saw they'd drifted far offshore. Alarmed, she tried to touch the sea floor with her feet.

Nothing.

And now they were both thrashing in the rip tide, trying to get a foothold. No words were exchanged, their jaws clenched shut against the churning. They knew what they were supposed to do, he'd coached her many times. Stay calm, don't fight the current, don't swim into the rip tide.

He'd already turned, was heading haltingly in the other direction. She saw him striving to align with the strip of beach they'd been on. She decided to try, she'll try to swim back, try to stay in a straight line, a parallel line, get back there, that's all.

Both raised their heads at every fourth stroke to check the shoreline in relation to their position, making sure they were on the correct trajectory. Both focused on their limbs slicing through the water, and on their solitary private terror that they might not make it, that what happened next was solely in their own hands. The dread of failing themselves both overwhelmed and propelled them.

He arrived first. He watched her from the dunes, a dark speck jerking against the silver-grey surface. By the time he'd dressed, she was halfway up the beach, head down, arms x-ed across her breasts. When she reached him she said nothing, started to dress, taking time over zippers, collars, cuffs.

'God, that was something!' he said.

She replied on a sharp inbreath. 'Yep.'

On the way back to the car, she said, 'You okay, then?' and they both knew her intention was to mark the chasm that had just opened up between them, to underline it, the sudden, clear realization that, caught in the rip tide, neither of them had spared one thought for the other.

The relationship didn't last much longer. In the years following, in their individual lives, they lied about the event, recounting it as if they swam to shore side by side, arms beating the water together like synchronized clocks until they were both safely on dry ground. Eventually, neither of them recounted the story at all.

***

Three am, a half-arsed moon, they're driving home through the drizzle, drunk. He's found her pearlescent blue-grey nail varnish in the glove compartment, Misty Dawn! just the trick! and is blowing loudly on his badly painted fingernails. Passing the strand, the car lights catch two white discs reflecting out at them. A dog?

Something about this hidden presence stirs him. (Recently he's been preyed upon by an irrational certainty there's some ghostly being tracking him.)

Then he remembers the local dogging rumours, and their recent dare. Perfect.

'Pull in,' he says, 'let's go walkies.'

'What's the magic word?'

'Christ, just pull in,' he says, twisting the steering wheel and gouging the pearl varnish.

In the dunes, they try to get their bearings. Car park empty, beach empty, no happy-slappy doggers tonight. Fuck it. Galway city still smoulders in the eastern sky. And ahead, across the bay, tiny lights on the coast of Clare.

'Shshsht,' she says, though they'd both been silent. 'Hear that?'

There's an animal yelping somewhere.

'A fox,' she says, 'a beautiful creature. Bet that's the eyes we saw in the ditch.'

'I dunno, sounds more like a dog to me. Maybe it's some wild dogging activity.'

'That's a fox, sweetheart. Calling out to its mate. Shshsht.'

'Shusht yerself. A dog, or doggers. Take your pick.'

The animal calls out again, a series of shrieks.

They sit in the dune's marram grass. He knows she's looking at him; he pictures himself in her eyes.

He straightens his back, touches his mouth, waits for her to lean in. Maybe now is a good time. He'll give her one lasting, sweet kiss, and then he'll tell her. The age gap, look, it's not working. She'll be upset, humiliated, he'll stay calm, respectful, willing to talk her through it. She'll refuse to engage. She'll drive back to their flat without him and, by the time he walks home, she'll have gotten used to it, will want out, will want to be the one leaving. With a bit of luck she may even have packed her stuff by then. He'll take over the lease. Could all be sorted by midweek.

She settles her head on his shoulder, picks at a seam repair she'd made to his shirt. The sea gripes low over its own pebbles. He rolls his shoulder away.

'Need to stretch.'

'Sorry, stretch away.'

He stands legs apart, extends his arms, swivels from the waist.

'You're like a helicopter about to take off,' she says, lying down into the marram. She spreads her arms cruciform.

'Hilarious. Want to hear a joke?'

'Sure.'

'About voodoo.'

'Sure.'

'Okay. So, if a doll, if you look into the eyes of a voodoo doll, of your voodoo doll …'

'Wait, what d'you mean "your doll"? Like, you own it but you're trying to stick needles in someone else?'

'No, sorry, my bad, the doll is you, you have it in your hands, for some reason, your own doll …'

'So, you've yourself in your hands?'

'Yeah, your own doll, and you're looking into its eyes, and, this is more of a riddle than a joke to be fair, so, if you're looking into its eyes, what would, wait, start again. What would happen if …'

'Look, let's go swimming, give me the punchline on the way.'

'It's not a punchline kind of thing but yeah, you do you.'

'What does that even mean, you do you,' she says, hauling herself from where she'd sprawled out prone, 'it makes no sense.' She undresses, snapping the air with each piece of clothing before throwing them on a pile at her feet. 'Furthermore, FYI, neither does the phrase my bad. Both grammatically incorrect. And not in a good way.'

She's naked, one step ahead of him. As she walks towards the tide, he slides down the dune, back towards a clump of ox-eye daisies at the edge, and grabs a fistful. He'll give them to her after the talk. They don't look like much now, but they'll be something when they open up in the morning.

He balls his clothes with hers, leaves the flowers on top, stumbles after her. She's waiting in the tide, hands on hips.

The water feels about the same as the air. When they're chest-deep, they float, splaying limbs. Starfish. He remembers the crucifix she made of herself on the marram. When her hand searches for his, he offers it. He hears the animal yelp again but this time it seems so far away it barely exists. Maybe it is people fucking. Class.

close your eyes to fix it here, a story, silver-tipped waves captured solid

The water shifts. For the first time, he notes the little licks of warning, the legion of tongues beginning to lash as one round his limbs. Spooked, he looks up. They've drifted far offshore. Shit, a bastard rip tide.

And now he's thrashing in the water, trying to pull himself back. He knows what he's supposed to do. Stay calm, don't fight the current. Swim parallel to shore until you're out of the rip tide. Then arc your way back to solid ground. For fuck's sake she's grasping for him, hands pawing the water, pug eyes fixed on him, lips pulled back chin jutting forward like a fucking puppy dog. 'Just swim!' he shouts, and turns, allowing the current to pull him from her. He curves his way towards the beach. Just once he hears her calling out.

When he reaches shore, he looks back. Where is she. He scans the horizon, everything quiet, streaks of dawn now visible to the east. She'll be grand. Might've reached land somewhere else, might've scrambled up the rocks at Cloosh, or drifted on towards Mutton Island. Christ, that's at least five kay away. At fucking least. How far out were they anyway? Not that far, they weren't past Cloosh Head surely.

He plods back to their belongings, gets dressed. He starts to fold her clothes away before realizing what he's doing. Maybe there's people watching. Doggers. Probably hiding in the dunes. Saw the whole thing. Watching him now. He gets to his feet, calls out towards the dark sea. Then again, louder, his hands splayed rigid either side of his mouth, fingers pointing skyward like pearl-tipped exclamation marks. 'Hey!' he shouts, and again, 'hey where are you!' because he doesn't know what else to do.

***

Three am, we were driving home. We saw discs glowing by the strand, so we pulled into the car park, to walk the dunes, to suck on some cold sea air.

Parking under the lone lamp post, we laughed about the dogging rumours. Wouldn't it be funny if we came across some fuckery. Yes, wouldn't that have been something.

On the dunes, we pulled greasy fistfuls of marram, scattered them behind us, some Hansel and Gretel thing, how to get back home, how to return (we didn't want to go home) (we were hoping to find people making El-Oh-Vee-EE, just for us). Our feet sank, cool sand filled our shoes, it felt good.

A yelping fox in a far-off field saw us standing there, and fled. The ocean grumbling over its worn pebbles reminded us of ourselves (we didn't want to be reminded). We stripped, then on into the waves.

The water felt no different than the air. We pushed past the little tongues lashing warnings at us (get back, back). We kept going, then floated, holding hands, X-X.

(close our eyes and fix it here, silver waves trapped solid)

This water shifted beneath us.

And on shore, what?

The yelp, so far away it barely exists (what was it, was it tomorrow).

This water shifted and we were not where we should be and we were trying to get back to what we were, but this keen, we found no foothold and our limbs, their sad frenzy, remember, but the water's no different than the air, and we left our limbs behind and we left our pink lungs behind and the cold ocean got into us and we were left behind is what it was.

***

Three am and we'll finally be heading homeward, spent. But when the beams catch something by the strand, we'll decide to pull in.

The sea will beckon us, gurgling baby-soft. When water whispers round our ankles, we'll keep walking. When water reaches the tender heat of our armpits, it'll seem that we've crossed a threshold. We'll let the waves rock us, forgive everything.

and you're trying to write about that last night you spent together in Silver Strand, and you've chosen to present the idea of tapetum lucidum in the eyes of nocturnal animals, trying to do the inexplicable justice, this miracle of a thin iridescent lining laying just behind the retina, a sheath that glows when light shines on it, reflecting back directly along the

light path, an echoing disc enabling night vision, and
without which clear sight would be impossible

and you're closing your eyes to picture a creature,
hiding in a hedgerow
on a damp spring night, to bear silent witness to it
there, hiding
from the overwhelming beams of an advancing car

a creature trying to get to the other side
trying to go back, back to its mate
and at the back of your eyes
can you find forgiveness

SKY AN IRIS

Three barrettes jut from Eily's mouth. Bathroom light humming in the dawn, she coils her plait into a silvered black bun at her nape. Her teenage son Cassius stands behind her, watching her in the mirror, covering one eye with his hand, then the next.

That what you're wearing to town, Cass?

Yep.

How 'bout your jeans instead of your shorts? You're a big boy now.

Nah.

Well, tie back your hair and go eat some muesli. Don't forget to screw the lid back on good and tight.

Her phone bleeps full charge from the hall stand below. She heads downstairs, pushes her arms through her husband's coat slumped damp over the banister where he left it earlier when he came in from tending the mare. It's still warm. She tips her fingers in the holy water font by the front door and sprinkles the framed photograph above it: her mother and father holding hands across a gleaming tractor engine at the Galway Ploughing Championships. She inherited the house and land from them after they died within three months of each other. The youngest sibling, she'd been the only one who promised not to leave.

Outside, the motion-detector light flashes on, illuminating the pea-gravel farmyard and the colour-coded rows of recycling bins where a slurry tank used to be. The air is still weighted with night; she feels it, ice across the forehead. Sinking her chin into the coat's musky collar, she pulls out the cart then fetches Bessie from the plywood stall in the garage beside her husband's car. Two of the mares look out the stable doors as she walks the doe-eyed ass to the yard and hitches her to the cart. She secures bit in mouth, the animal rolling its tongue over the chilly metal. In the dark dawn sky, shafts of car light shoot across rushes in waterlogged fields: neighbours striking out to Roscommon for work, or on to Galway to their cloud-computing jobs in IBM, Oracle, SAP, Cisco. Narrowing her eyes, she evaluates the heavy clouds in the distance, then pats the animal's rump before bending to inspect each oiled hoof.

She's never learnt to drive. That particular freedom, she's decided, is not for her. She understands this puts pressure on her husband. She's told him she just could never picture herself behind a wheel, reversing, indicating. And if she can't picture it, she can't do it. Her will is strong, he knows enough not to challenge it. Both of them having been brought up on the land, he accepts her preference for the dependable strive of a working animal, the simple dialect of whistles and clicks, snorts and whinnies.

Since early adulthood, since just before she met him, she has struggled to trust any car's set mechanism, has considered their machinations daunting. The language itself unnerves her – coolant, clutch, alternators, the mystery of batteries, of spark plugs. To steer, to aquaplane, the stark rev of engine in the stillness of a country lane, the slick acceleration, the slip-slap of wiper blades on a sodden stormy morning, the dry hum of heater, the navy flash of school uniform, the slither of braking tyres, a thin scream.

The trip to Roscommon this morning is unavoidable; she needs to sell her week-old chicks at the artisan market. There are always fresh-faced young couples, IT recruits eager to start a self-sustaining life in the country, beginning with a chicken coop which they'll learn is no deterrent to foxes or minks. Whatever chicks Eily has left, she'll sell quarter-price as fresh feed to the Captive Raptor Research Centre on the Roscommon–Sligo border.

She has watched over the eggs in her henhouse incubator, has hearkened to the little beaks tip-tip-tapping from inside their shells. She has moved each of the newly hatched to the receiving box above, warmed with an infrared bulb. She has fed to the pigs the eggs that remain silent, holding every one of the shrouded puzzles up to the light before throwing it into the swill bucket.

At seven days old, the hatched need to go. In the henhouse beside the stables, Eily packs the chirping chicks into two cardboard boxes and carries them out to place them in the cart. His hair hanging lank over his face, Cassius stands by the cartwheel, kicking the spokes, listing at each strike:

Silkies. White an' black.
Phoenix. Silver an' gold.
Rhode Island Red. Red.

Born too early, born too late, it's held Cassius shouldn't have been born at all. Why had he come, five weeks premature, to a delighted Eily, a first-time mother at forty-five? To a father who'd spent years yearning for a child he knew could never happen, knew it even before, still childless after their third wedding anniversary, the doctor took him out of earshot and explained to him about fickle genetics, about the treason of hereditary infertility, about how he should consider carefully before deciding whether to tell his fragile wife.

After the birth, it had been a slow dawning for them: Cassius wasn't going to follow the template. At three, he struggled to walk, to feed himself. At five, only his parents could comprehend him. At eight, it was understood he could never attend school, never sit in line, never use a pen without smearing the page with shocks of indigo, never understand a computer keyboard or join in song without slapping hands to eyes, wailing. On his last journey home from school, he'd recited the classroom songs, cocooned beside his father in their car. He was homeschooled from then, trailing his parents around their organic farm.

Eily's husband can't drive them to town, their eldest mare having gone into labour last night. It's proving to be a difficult delivery. She has to face the journey alongside Cassius without him. She checks the battery on her phone then refreshes once more the local weather site. She cuts a thin rod from a sally tree.

They're no more than three kilometres up the Roscommon road when Cassius lunges at the reins. Eily flicks the sally rod, snatching the leather back.

No, Cassie! It's dangerous, sit back down, good boy.

I want a bring Bessie a town!

Watch me do it.

Nah, Mum! Let me!

Stop! You'll frighten Bessie. If you're good, I'll let you take her home. Now watch me work the reins. Watch Bessie's mouth, her ears moving. Watch her hooves, which one leads. Listen to my clicks, she knows them.

But Cassius has turned away towards the open back of the cart, staring sullen through his tangled locks at the retreating road.

Eily's husband is as charmed and wary of her as he is of his black-eyed child. He both monitors and embraces their peculiarities: his son's pressing inventories of minutiae, his wife's terror of a darkening sky. Just before he met and married her, there'd been an incident during a morning thunderstorm. She'd been a giddy front-seat passenger being driven home from an all-night party, her own twenty-first in Roscommon. Water had built up between the tyres and the road. There was no traction. Unchecked, the car would respond to neither steering nor braking. A neighbour, the young McLaughlin girl walking to school, had been killed.

Having rejected her parents' devotion to prayer in her teenage years, he watched her take it up again not long after this incident, embracing it with more fervour than her parents ever had. His wife's day now seems hinged around appeals for redemption – the morning prayer, the evening rosary with him and Cassius. He stoops to her rituals, however senseless he deems them to be.

During the day, he spends most of his time outdoors, tending to his animals, while she darts between henhouse, polytunnel and home. His son shadows from a distance, moving at regular intervals between them both, following some internal clock.

The family of three come together in the evening, and he reunites finally with his wife at night, their bedroom door ajar. Their son lies awake in the adjoining room, his door jammed open with a three-legged Buckaroo. Every night, his lanky teenage body reaching from headboard to base, Cassius lists his neighbours' names, counties of origin, dates of birth, zodiac signs, eye colours.

Mister Eugene McLaughlin.

The County Roscommon.

March thirty-first, one-nine-six-five.

Aries.

Black, an' gold flash.

As their cart passes the jennet's field, the crossbreed whinnies. The sound ends in an ass's bray, a throwback to its mother. Cassius stands, faces the sound.

What? What you want, Blood? You want a be going down the road?

Quit with the shouting, Cass! And sit back down before you fall off, there's a good lad.

Cassius covers his mouth with his hand. His mother taps the space behind her with the sally rod.

Come on, Cassie, don't stand in a moving cart. And don't draw that poor creature over, it's gone bad.

From behind his palm, Cassius calls out to the animal, a high, lingering whistle. The crossbreed flattens its long ears and gallops towards the hawthorn ditch, shaking its mohawk mane, its swish tail high. Cassius swings his arms out.

Whaat! What you waant!

Straining on the reins, Bessie searches the jennet's field, trying to see past her blinkers. She stops sudden mid-trot, and veers in towards the ditch. The boxes slide across the tilted cart. A panic of chirps rises but the stiff cardboard lids remain folded. Eily yanks the reins.

Cassius! What kind of a bloody fool are you! Sit down, before I wallop the nonsense out of you, and by Christ I will!

Pulling the ass back onto the road, Eily whacks the dark cruciform stripe along the animal's spine with the sally rod. Bessie counters with a sharp tug before trotting on.

Move those boxes back up here behind me, Cass, and sit yourself down right now please.

Cassius sees the despair in the jennet, its dark-eyed stare from behind the white hawthorns. He wipes his nose with his sleeve and settles between his mother and the boxes.

Eily promises her god daily that she'll carry with grace the heavy blessing he has bestowed after her years of silent pleading. Every evening, before bed, she has her husband and son join her to recite the rosary: the Joyful, the Luminous, the Sorrowful or the Glorious Mysteries, depending on the day. Facing her St Anne and Child statuette placed on top of the television, she leads and they follow.

We fly to Thee, O Virgin of Virgins, our Mother. To Thee do we come, before Thee we stand, sinful and sorrowful.

Head bowed, her husband mouths the incantations. Listening to his wife's voice skim soft through the words, he hovers over those silent spaces in between, over truths hidden beneath the worn prayers. He has forgiven her a long time ago.

Cassius pulls threads from his shirt and pokes the tiny honeycomb of speaker holes on the side of the television. The sound is muted; lips form words on the screen, opening and closing, stretching and pouting. He waits for them to sync with his mother's prayer; they always do, eventually, even if just for a few seconds. He drones 'prayfrus, prayfrus, prayfrus', only falling into line with his father at the conclusion, when saints are invoked.

O Holy St Anthony.

Pray for us.

Saint Therese of Lisieux.

Pray for us.

At the end, Eily presents the statuette to them. Her husband's lips brush over St Anne's feet. Her son blesses himself with both hands, slapping forehead, chest, shoulders. Her heart cramps as he kisses St Anne's plaster head and strokes the veil-draped head of the Child.

Several cars pass them along the road, drivers waving cautiously out the window, buckled children staring motionless. Eily looks straight ahead, lifting one finger in curt greeting from her tightly balled fist around the reins. Bessie trots on, ears swivelling, grey head nodding. Cassius taps the cardboard lids in time with the hoofbeats.

Red-orange-yellow-green-blue-indigo-violet.

Eily stiffens.

Where? Where's the rainbow, Cassius?

There. Behind. Over Blood's field. And look a big black sky round it, Mum. A big black lid round the lot of us, and us in a big pot, and not a one of us can get out.

She hears the first heaving trundle of thunder. Pulling Bessie up, she stands, listening, searching the sky, her hand trembling on her son's shoulder. The next swell of thunder blasts overhead as a flare of lightning bursts, its crackled light fizzing around them.

Home! We're going home! We've to go home, Cassius!

She pulls hard on the rein, turning back. The twisting bit cuts Bessie's lip. Grinding teeth, the animal shakes her stiff mane, shunts back and forth in a series of awkward moves, and breaks into a trot homeward. Eily's phone bleats in her pocket.

She'd known Cassius was touched by the hand of her god long before her husband did. She'd noticed early the baby's closed stare, the limp puppet hands, the slack mouth. She'd kissed her tiny son, caressed him, crooned to him, cajoled him, but never once had the infant broken into a smile, never once had her child slipped a hand in hers, never nestled in her lap or answered her rhymes: 'Hickory Dickory Dock, the mouse ran up the? … Cassie … Ran up the? …'

As he grew, she'd fixed on her son's darkening eyes, seeking to steer them towards some shade of blue. The halcyon blue of a clear and cloudless day or, God, please, her husband's raw blue, his iris a pure sky.

But as the years passed and her son's eyes continued to darken, she suffered Cassius' impenetrable stare as a just yoke. Hadn't her prayers been sufficiently answered, lying under McLaughlin in a neighbouring shed? She'd been his childhood crush, she'd always known how he'd longed for her. Brittle as their covenant was, McLaughlin got a retribution he was marginally satisfied with, a flimsy redress for his dead sister mangled by a car years before. And Eily got her child. Neither could ask for more.

For the first few years, she waited for her husband to hold the child up to the light and see within, see right through, to her. After a while, for both child and husband, she learned to take one day at a time.

She tackled her son on each misconception as it happened.

You can't eat your dinner with a bread knife.

For why?

You can't leave your bed at night to wander among the horses.

For why?

You can't put the chicks in the kettle.

For why, Mum?

Another swollen belt of thunder, another splinter of lightning, a streak of rain sweeps over the rushing cart. The box lids ping under the fat drops, the cardboard darkening, the chicks silent. The phone starts to bleat from her coat pocket again. She looks down. Cassius makes a grab for the reins.

I'll takes Bessie home!

Cassius! No!

You says I could!

Stop!

She catches her son's wet thigh with a slicing lash of the rod. Cassius shrieks, rolling into a ball. Slowly, he begins a low howl, hiding his face.

Jesus Christ, Cassius, shut up!

Her teeth bared against the downpour, Eily belts Bessie, the whack raising a thin stripe of rain from the animal's pelt. The ass stumbles into a canter, ears back, muzzle into the torrent, hooves flittering tarmac pellets onto her pale velvet belly. Reins gripped, plait slapping behind her, Eily turns her face to the sky.

I'm sorry! Sorry for the want in me!

They've reached the jennet's field. Beyond the ditch, on the other side of the hawthorns, the crossbreed gallops in line with Bessie through the lashing rain. The cart wheels buck, rattling over the road. The boxes clatter on the cart bed, walloping into Cassius's smarting thigh, a raging welt glowing there where the rod had struck him. He kicks out. One of the boxes slides to the open back of the cart. With the next jolt it falls off. The sodden cardboard splits open on hitting the road. Cassius gawps as the chicks are strewn over the tarmac, into the ditch, fluttering their hopeless wings. He grabs the remaining box and pulls it to his chest, folding long limbs around it. 'Prayfrus, prayfrus, prayfrus,' he whispers to the hatchlings within as he loses sight of the scattered left behind opening and closing their tiny beaks to the falling rain, eye beads blinking.

The cart swerves into the yard and Eily jerks the ass to a stop. Her husband is waiting for them, phone in hand. He'd left the mare, a sleek newborn foal glistening on its spindly legs by her side, when he'd heard the first thunder growl.

He sees the steam rise off his Bessie. Head drooping, the animal rattles the bit, a dribble of bloodied foam at her lip. Eily jumps off, flinging the rod to the ground.

Christ! Just a bit up the road and a fucking thunderstorm! Out of fucking nowhere!

Rain drips from her. Her cheeks flash red, like a child's. He cups her chin.

Eily, you're home now.

Fucking hell!

Why didn't you answer your phone? I could've picked you up. Cass is old enough to take Bessie home himself. You know that. This is what we've been teaching him.

Cassius lifts his head from his knees, looks to his father. Eily rages on.

Don't get me started about Cassius! Or that half-baked Bessie! Christ!

Look, go on inside. Make some coffee. I'll be in later, when I'm finished with the mare. She's just foaled, a beautiful sorrel filly. All good so far. Think of a name.

Eily wipes her face with a sleeve.

And that fucking lunatic jennet you sold McLaughlin spooked the shit out of Bessie, she nearly had us spilled onto the middle of the road with trying to get to it!

Go inside, Eily. Go on.

The sky flickers silver. She shrieks. Slapping her hands over her ears, she runs stooped towards the house.

He helps his son off the cart. 'Good lad, there's my good lad' is all he can say. Cassius walks slumped, shielding the cardboard box from the rain, and disappears inside the henhouse.

He turns back to Bessie, unyokes her, leads her into her plywood stall in the corner of the garage. He dries her with a blanket, muttering to her, scattering straw beneath her. She smells the foal off him, licks at his hands.

He thinks of the jennet, crossbreed offspring of Bessie and his Connemara stallion. He remembers the night he delivered the heavy foal, Cassius at his side. 'What name will we give it,' he asked his son. 'Blood,' said Cassius, 'that's Bessie's lovely Blood.' He remembers the months following; the peculiar long-legged colt skipping an awkward delight behind Bessie in the field.

The crossbreed is infertile. He'd told his neighbour to have it castrated after he sold it to him. But Eugene McLaughlin, an unreasonable man not given to taking instruction, paid little attention. He understood McLaughlin harboured an anger since his youth. He'd lost his only sibling when she was nine years old; his childhood neighbour and some townie drunk had ploughed her down. It had taken McLaughlin some time to forgive Eily, but he'd come round in the end.

McLaughlin bought the jennet to amuse his brood of dark-eyed youngsters. A sterile stallion was of no use, he'd been advised, a gelding would be easier to handle, safer for the kids. But he neglected the counsel, and the children grew frightened of the flighty animal. Now, two years on, his children keep their distance. It spends its time isolated in its field, gone mad with the lonesome fury. No one should attempt to go near it, McLaughlin has warned them all, no man nor beast. It's worse it's getting, but what can we do now. The poor creature carries its own trouble, leave it alone, leave it be, he says.

The rain beats off the galvanized roof of the garage. Bessie places her muzzle in his hand. He's tired, hardly slept all night. Leaning against her neck, he brushes the tar flecks from her belly and watches through the open stall door as Cassius leaves the henhouse, walks back up the road, and disappears into the rain, a skipping rope stuffed into his shirt pocket. He knows there's little point in calling out to him, where you going, what you doing, when will you be back. Murmuring to Bessie, he rises and heads into the house to get Eily. He wants to bring her to the tiny newborn foal, her favourite thing in the world, brighten her up a bit.

Later, they'll be hand in hand inside the mare's stall, the sun's rays on the little sorrel filly. The mare's ears will flicker sudden towards the road. They'll follow her implication and stand together at the stable door, listening. They'll hear a distant, discordant beat. Soon they'll see their son skittering back towards home, his dirty hair whipping behind him. They'll see him lead the jennet, trotting and bucking alongside, whinnying and braying, its ragged hooves pealing on the shiny road. They'll see his old skipping rope tied loose around the animal's neck, one handle bouncing off steaming withers, the other held fast in his hand. They'll see the bulging pockets of his shirt, the left one full of dead chicks, milky eyes hardening, the right one sheltering three chirping siblings, little beaks pulling at the loose threads.

SEA EAGLE SONATA

ask him if he'd like a top-up

customers aren't offered top-ups for
tea, top-ups are for coffee, tea is a once-
off thing, a sacred thing, a beginning
a middle an end kind of thing, it has
parameters beyond which it cannot—

*shut up / just go out there and ask him / he
looks wrecked / more wrecked than usual*

The elderly baker sticks his head through the hanging beads separating kitchen from café. It's early morning. The place is empty but for the young man sitting at a table by the window, scrolling through his phone.

'Would you like a top-up for your tea there?'

'Eh, I'm grand, man. Thanks, though.'

'Thought so. Maybe a drop of hot water? Or hot water and another teabag? Or is that just a new tea altogether? Ha ha! Like, when does the old cup actually become a new cup? Or is a cup of tea the tea or the cup? Ha ha! Wild stuff.'

'Yeah, I'm grand, thanks a mill.'

he doesn't want to chat / look at the state of him / don't overstep the mark

'Look, I'll leave you alone, don't mind me, I'm an awful man for rambling on, as you well know!'

'No worries, sham. Sorry I'm not much craic this morning.'

'If you need a top-up, just shout. I'll be foostering around, as usual, with me big flowery apron on, ha ha! Do you want to make a swan? Give it another go?'

'I'm sound, for the moment.'

go back into the kitchen / sort out the éclairs

'Okay, I'll be in the kitchen, I've to sort out éclairs and things. Shout if you change your mind. About the top-up. Or the swan.'

quit talking about top-ups / the éclairs are beginning to curl in the oven

'Anyways, righto, I'm off, son. Back shortly.'

for the love of God don't call him son

'Grand. I'll shout if I need anything. Thanks.'

The young man draws his chair closer to the table, turns back to his phone. The baker returns to the windowless kitchen, sits on a stool by the warm oven, addresses the shelf of tiny origami birds across from him.

christ, did you see his face, eyes like
piss-holes

yes

should have left him in peace, that's
what he comes in here for

and stop with the origami lessons

yes, you're probably right, he's not a child,
he's getting handy at it though, remember

yesterday morning, nearly there but
the swan's wings were fecked, we'll work
on that today, are the buns baked

éclairs / they are

good

listen / something's up with that young lad

I always listen, should I take them
éclair-buns out

so you do / yes take them out

I do because you never shut up,
put the cream on is it

*let them cool / whip the cream / microwave the
chocolate on low*

wouldn't shut up when you were here,
won't shut up now, let them cool then dollop
cream into them and slap on some chocolate,
it's grand, there's always YouTube

you'll be fine / you're doing great

am I now, am I, I can see your beautiful
hands doing it great

don't / no point

and your arms white with flour, the hairs
standing on them with the cold from the door
open onto the Dublin docklands morning, you
were some handsome woman

no point remembering

and the odd stroller walking by with a dog
or pram or bike, gawking in, smelling the hot
sweetness—

what's the point

—and after, like nothing happened, decorating
the cakes, all business—

nothing happening

—bent over the trays, tongue tipping out
the side of your mouth, squeezing sweet
cream from that rubbery thing

the pastry bag

like baby uilleann pipes, that rubber bag,
lines of cream swirling from it onto the cakes
and the buns and the everything

pointless / I'm gone

you were something else

I was

us locking hands spinning round
the floor like, like a mad, a gyroscope
or something—

a gyroscope is it

—when the shutters were down,
not letting go till we hit the ground

room swirling behind us

and then, eyes reeling in our heads

wild whirlwinds

the two of us

the two of us

hard to believe, where are you gone

where

where is that pastry lung thing

in the cutlery drawer

I miss you

yes

seven months eleven days, two hundred
and twenty-five days total

you need to talk to people

correct

talk to real people

I know

to that young man / the content moderator as he calls himself

yes

open up

yes

without whingeing

okay

he could do with it too

probably

a bit of warmth

how can I talk to people when all I hear is
you warbling on about warmth and cream

don't forget to turn the oven off

yes

whip caster sugar into the cream

righto

gently / you're not flailing a dead pony

it's flogging a dead horse

make some dark some milk chocolate / the young go for the dark

yes

and do not call him son / he's somebody's son / not ours

not ours indeed

don't get into all that / talk about climate change / rise of AI

origami, the origins of—

or the lad's job / something's wrong

something's not right

talk to him about it / you're good with people

if you say so

bring éclairs / one dark one milk

The baker centres an intricate paper doily on a plate and arranges two éclairs there. Putting the plate on a tray, he adds a rolled cloth napkin. He picks up a tiny origami swan from his collection, perches it on the napkin, and goes into the café. The young man is staring out the window, his back to the kitchen. The gold-lettered name of some minor football club stretches across his thin shoulders.

'Here we are, straight from the oven! On the house, my friend!'

'Jesus, lovely job, thanks, man. Home away from home.'

no don't sit with him / just put down the plate

'My pleasure. You're always welcome here. And cripes, you've been working hard! Ten-hour shifts, through the night, one night after the other—'

great he'll think you're a stalker

'—don't worry, I'm no stalker! It's just that I spot you going in across the road ...'

a stalker then

'… I can see you heading up the stairwell, before the time-delay light switch turns off … because, you see, I'm awake for a while meself at night, to set the oven for morning before I traipse on off to me leaba upstairs.'

'Ah right. A busy man.'

'Sourdough, ciabatta, rye. A fistful of poppy seeds on everything, is the trick apparently. Then the éclairs in the morning. Swift learning curve for this here gent! The missus …'

don't bring me up

'… You see, the missus used to do it all.'

The young man leans back in his chair, zips his sports jacket up to his chin, sinks his mouth in behind the polyester, stuffs his hands in the pockets. The baker continues.

'Yeah, ha ha! There was a missus, believe it or not! And then, you see, in the morning, I do watch you emerging bleary-eyed from across the way. Up all night, you are. Fair play to you, fair play.'

'Sure there's two of us in it.'

'Righto, I'm getting you a fresh cup, back in a sec. Look, there, on the napkin, another swan for you while you're waiting. Have a go again at copying it. Trick is, start by figuring out how it's made. Unfold it first. Work backwards. Then make it again. And dig in to the éclairs, get some meat on those bones!'

'Sound, sham, will do.'

The young man unzips his jacket, leans forward, elbows on the table. As the baker returns to the kitchen, he hears a ping. He looks back through the beads. The lad checks his phone, mutes, picks up the origami swan, stares at it for a while, rotates it in his palm, returns it to the table. He straightens his back and with his mouth hanging open rubs both eyes with balled fists, like a drowsy child. The baker's breath catches. He turns back, sits once more by the oven.

*

meat-on-bones was inappropriate

didn't bother him, think he likes
the bit of mothering

maybe

look at him, head bent to the swan

he's spent from work

imagine sitting in an office
all night, open-plan as they call it,
tethered to a screen, everyone lined up
like horses in stalls

all night

imagine having to decide what's right
and what's wrong for the rest of us, that's a
woeful amount of pressure for a young lad,
barely a man, a woeful amount of
the world's crap to take on

it is

some of the godawful things he's had
to watch, the few he's told me about,
dear God, remember

don't

can't get them out of my head

no don't

the young lad backed up to a
black flag, hands tied with barbed wire,
wide-eyed at the camera, ordered to kneel
in a language he doesn't understand

stop / bad to dwell here

somebody's son

think of the two of us

him across the way working all night while the
two of us sleep, or at least while I sleep and you,
you willowy thing, curled up in my dreams

still in your dreams

do you dream, a dream dreaming

you're doing great

am I

the tea / bring him more tea

The baker returns to the young man. The éclairs are gone.

'Here you go, my friend, a top-up in your hand whether you ordered it or not! That's the sort of me! Can't bear to see a man with a cold cup. Well now, you've unfolded the bird but it can't be said you've put it back together again, now can it! Ha ha! You're flummoxed! Flummoxed by a paper bird!'

'Completely flummoxed, man.'

check the milk

'Plenty of milk in the jug for you there. And listen, you can do it. Take your time. Morning traffic beginning to build outside. Bumper to bumper. And they'll all rush back this evening. Work, work, work.'

'Work, work, work, and more work. It's all a fucking balls. Sorry, I'm wrecked.'

ask him about time off

'Do you get much holliers? Time to clear the mind of all that online muck? Head off anywhere nice? With the missus ...'

don't assume a missus

'... or a friend, or even by yourself? I spent a set of days on the Isle of Skye, seven months ago now it must have been. Been there before but all on me ownio this time, dodging the seagulls, walking the hills and hollows by the shore. Fecking beautiful, pardon mon french-ay. Just me and the gulls. Or *the gulls and I*, as someone would have corrected me once. I got a bunch of pics printed out when I came back, to make an album, something you can hold. It's upstairs in the bedroom, will I get it? You can have a look? At Skye?'

*

Something about the old baker's printed pictures; the crappiness of the paper, the fading colours, the occasional fat red thumb in the corner, the blurred seagulls in flight. Something about the lopsided selfies, about how sure the baker was that these limp, these bleached photos of the Isle of Skye would somehow be meaningful to you.

And something about a large black rock on a headland jutting out to sea like a clenched fist, *THE BLACK ROCK* written and underlined at the bottom of the photo, a few misshapen love hearts scrawled at the end. It reminded you of Ben Bulben, and the time the stone mountain summoned you, the time you spent there alone on the crest, alone with the stray.

You didn't go home to your flat in Drumcondra that morning, to your game console at the foot of your bed, the stack waiting on your bedside stand: *Skyrim*, *Valheim*, *Minecraft*.

You left the café and took the Luas straight to Connolly Station, bought a ticket for the Belfast Enterprise. Slept on the train. Swallowed hot sweet tea on the ferry to Stranraer, milky coffee on the train to Glasgow. Flicked through your phone until the battery died then stared out past your strobed reflection at the plunging night as you were scuttled over the tracks to Inverness. By the time you made it to a Kyle of Lochalsh dawn, you'd used up your meagre rainy-day cache of sterling which you'd always kept folded in your wallet, just in case.

You walked, hunched into spring mizzle, across the bridge to the Isle of Skye. Burly seagulls criss-crossed in front of you, muttering like they'd been kept waiting. The hood of your Sligo GAA jacket was tied against the damp morning air. You knew this weather. No one was around to read the county's motto arched across your shoulders, *Land of Heart's Desire*, the once-gold lettering fading back into the striped black and white polyester, the golden shell motifs peeling off. 'Heart's Desire calling,' you told the gulls.

You spotted a lone taxi parked up. You described the black rock you'd seen in the baker's photograph. 'Ah, Scorrybreac,' she said, and accepted a twenty-euro note to drop you to a car park in Portree Bay, instructing you on how to reach the headland from there.

As you climbed the trail, sea on your right, the sun came out. You thought of your job, how the others would probably have covered for you last night though some of them don't even know your name. You thought of your half-litre of fortified milk sitting in the fridge beside the Red Bulls and energy bars. You thought of the communal packets of Polo mints, always two or three floating around. You thought of the tiny staff room: microwave, small fridge, table, chairs, four sockets. And you thought of the baker, wondered whether this morning's absence had yet been noted by him.

The sea was calm. You were alone on the trail. You kept going. When you recognized his beloved Black Rock jutting out from the headland before you, you sat down on the damp heather, jacket in lap. You took a half-melted chocolate bar from the pocket and ate it, peeling strips of tin foil from the sweet gloop and letting them sail away one by one on the breeze. Slowly, you folded the purple paper wrapper into a tiny swan. It wasn't perfect, but it was close. Pleating the small wings upward, you flicked it over the cliff edge and watched it spiralling towards the waves. When you lost sight of it, you looked out to sea, blinking into the morning sun.

*

She soars on a thermal, talons tucked into her body. Her mate is behind, calling. The sleek finger-feathers at either end of her dark wingspan flicker upward in the soft wind. The Atlantic glisters below.

She twists her head, eyes her mate. Extending his talons in play, his white tail fans out to slow his flight. He beats his broad wings, twice, then glides once more. She folds one wing into herself, turning back swiftly to him. Meeting, they interlock talons and cartwheel downward together through the air. Wings lashing against the spin, their pale yellow eyes are fixed, sea and sky tumbling behind them.

Swooping apart just as they're about to hit water, their feathers skim the surface. After four shallow wingbeats over the waves, they tilt back towards each other. He rolls under, touching his talons to hers before scudding upwards. She follows, calling.

The cliff face looms. Their enduring eyrie of heather, juniper and driftwood nestles in a hollow there, shreds of seaweed and moss lining the inside.

She spots motion on the headland, banks sharp towards it. Sunlight is catching thin ribbons carried swirling on the wind. She draws nearer, focuses on a man releasing shiny inanimate strips into the air. Her eye follows the slivers of tin, determining their composition. Disinterested, she beats her wings to rise, and steadies onto a thermal once more. Her mate follows, silent.

Returning her gaze to the lone man, she watches him flick a small shape from him. Its folded purple manifests to her as a multitude of vivid shades, an alluring spectrum of amethysts and sapphires. Half-closing one wing, she dives down towards the falling form. When close to her mark, she establishes its inertness but is driven to catch it in her beak before twisting away upward. Her tongue probes the sugary pleated paper.

Rolling her eye back under its bony brow-ridge to the man exposed on the headland above their eyrie, she watches him staring up at her, his mouth dropping open. He stands, and a tangle of black, white and gold falls lifeless at his feet. He cries out to her, slowly extends his arms wide, yielding his bare throat, calling, benevolent, his body open, harmless.

Her waiting mate signals caution. She swings back up towards his open-winged silhouette hovering dark before the sun. Circling around him, she listens to the fading serenade from the prone man below, then pirouettes skyward, the sea air lifting her wings.

SIX FIELDS A WOOD A STREAM

Friday evening, I'm in the back of their daddy's Ford Cortina, The Twins either side of me, jingling with bracelets. Their older brother driving, thirty miles an hour, revs and Horslips, smoke rings, winking at me in the rear-view mirror. Their granny's rosary beads swinging when he brakes at every bend. There was no need to drive, it's still bright out, we could've easily walked. The Marian Hall is only about five or six fields, a scrappy wood and one slow stream away from our row of houses.

Things to Bear In Mind:

– The Twins can't stand the sight of me

- I've never been to a disco
- I can't stand the sight of the pair of them either
- I'm wearing my older brother's jeans (gone, last autumn, Melbourne, work visa)
- I've brought along some items, namely, a compass, a few quartz pebbles
- I need to be ready for some kind of slagging about this in school on Monday

The main reason we're squashed into the Cortina is that The Twins are afraid of cows and didn't want to get their new ankle boots mucky by trekking through the fields and woodland between our houses and the hall. Also, their brother is raring for any opportunity to get behind the wheel. He's a tremendous pain, hope to Christ he's not going to the disco too, probably not, he's doing his Leaving Cert exams in June, or at least he's supposed to be but not much sign of it on the cretin this April evening.

The Marian Hall Disco. The Disco Hall of Marrying. Can't believe I'm heading there. Can't believe I'm heading there with this pair. I'm pretending I don't know Mam asked them to take me. 'Would you girls ever take her along for the ride?' Hilarious. The ride. Poor Mam. 'Putting yourself out there is good for you,' says she, but I spent most of last summer outside and she wasn't exactly ecstatic about that. Ticks, skin burnt to a Tayto, stings, knees cracked open. Reason being, I got into bees, amazing amazing bees for my school's summer project. I took out every book about them from the library, then went looking for wild hives. I trekked into the fields and woods, seeing what was what. I took note of every hedge, tree, laneway, stream and ditch.

Fact 1: when a bee finds a good source of food, it races back to the hive and jigs like mad on the comb to show the rest of the gang where to go and how far. Each fancy dance move means something, 'it's over there, north-west, 190 yards, go, go!'

Fact 2: scientists once put a bowl of sugar-water on a boat anchored in the middle of a lake as an experiment on the poor bees. They wanted to see if the bees had any cop. So the scout bee finds the sugar-water and flies back to the hive to tell them all, 'There's food! It's in the middle of the lake but, I swear, there's good food!' Do you think the rest of the bees would believe her? Would they me shite. Not one of them flew to the middle of the lake because they were thinking *How could there be nectar there?* So they have cop alright, a type of cop, though the bee was telling the truth and not a single one of them fuzzy bastards listened.

Fact 3: bees can roam miles from their hive yet always find their way back. They like to do this between late morning and early afternoon, when it's warmish. They don't bother with roaming at night. It does get weird when it's dark, like you've walked through the mirror; everything's different, noises different, air different somehow. Different for humans that is, not for bees, they don't give a shite about weirdness, night or day. Come dark, they have the cop to cuddle up together and mind their babies and mind their queen and mind their own business.

Every year in May, before we break up for the holidays, the school asks each student to 'busy themselves' over the summer, finding out stuff about their locality that they can present to the other students come September. It's the annual school summer project. Last year, the theme was *Mapping Your Locality*. The Twins just mapped out their back garden, focusing on their famous vegetable patch with names of their prize vegetables attached to each row (they still don't know it was me and my brother who stole their best turnip when we were all little chislers). One moron plotted out his house's interior floor plan, two storeys, two diagrams. Another one drew her bedroom from different angles, 'Bird's-Eye Views Project', she titled it.

I did the bee project. A diorama, papier mâché on plywood, scale 1:5280, mapping an area radiating three miles outward from my home (a tiny white house placed in the centre, the other three houses in the row painted black, sorry Twins, it's just the way it had to be).

First I painted the fields green, the rivers blue, the roads grey, the woods brown, the marshes purple. I got miniature props from the model railway shop and placed the fences and hedges, the houses, sheds and pens, our old primary school and its fuchsia bush, all exactly where they really are. I posed myself in the wood behind my house, a tiny Little Red Riding Hood figurine I've had since childhood. I exed in red marker where each wild beehive was, at least the two I'd found on my treks, hidden in dead trees. To show each beehive's foraging area, I spray-painted adhesive then sprinkled fantastic glitter on top, silver for one, gold for the other. The two areas overlapped, both forage realms joining up easy like old friends meeting up at a fancy-dress party wearing the same sparkly costume.

In September, the entire school was summoned to come look at it. It was set up on a table in the canteen. The teacher told me I do cast my net wide, which is good. Everybody clapped (also good, sort of).

The Twins have been going to the Marian Hall Disco every second Friday evening for the past four months, since the local Youth Club kick-started the thing during the Christmas holidays. 'Some Fortnightly Fun to Occupy our Young Teens' announced the flyer that landed in our postbox. I'd say the pair are sorry now they were blowing to Mam about how great it was. 'Oh yeah, it's a lot of fun, everyone brings their LPs, everyone dances together.' *Jesus don't make us bring the freak, Jesus Mary, she can't come, are you having us on, are you having a laugh?*

<u>Things Found (so far) as Inspiration for my Next Summer Project</u>

- One pair of black patent shoes, ladies', discarded in field
- One perished doll, eyes missing, family of snails inside head
- Series of sword razor shells, far from shore (how/why?)
- One knotted birch branch, approximating a reef knot
- Several old clay pipes, most still working (tested)
- Two fivers, found in separate locations, both near water, on the exact same date

- Three hard-as-rock gingernut biscuits, perfect condition

So we land outside the Marian Hall. First sister gets out one side, second out the other, both bang the car doors shut, both scared to death they'll be stuck with me. The Wally up front starts sniggering and roars out the window at the first one that she forgot something on the back seat, 'don't leave that one sitting there staring at me like I'm her daddy'. She swings round and blasts at him, 'Be back here. Ten pm. Sharp. Thank you. Good night,' before click-clacking to the entrance on her ankle-boot heels, the other one behind her. They open the door and the sound of Geldof moaning about Mondays escapes before the door slams shut.

I have to hand it to her; that was marvellous. I look at The Wally, who's still watching me in the rear-view mirror. Clear as I can, I repeat, 'Be here at ten sharp goodnight' and add 'Wally' as I get out of the car. He doesn't say a word. I take a quartz pebble from my pocket, lean in his window and leave it on his knee. You never know.

<u>Things that DO NOT Happen When I Enter the Hall</u>

1. The music stops, a hush descends

2. Everyone applauds me warmly (those that are sitting, stand)
3. I amble through, greeting some with a tongue-click wink
4. The dancers part like the Red Sea, reaching out to touch me
5. The Twins beckon me to come join them

I walk in. The Boomtown Rats are concluding their rant. Turns out their plan is to shoot the day down. Interesting approach. The Twins have seeped into the crowd. There are some girls in the middle of the floor dancing, coloured lights spinning on the floor. There's a boy on stage by the red-velvet curtains, leaning over the record player to line up the next song. He's the older brother of someone I know from school. I wave, but he doesn't seem to recognize me. There are bunches of people scattered around talking. I nod at the ones I know, some nod back. So far so good.

I saunter to the hall's community notice board. It's a good move, there's loads to read: dates for Poker night, Set-dancing, Introduction to Aerobics, Rules and Regulations of The Hall (no horse-play please), newsprint cut-outs of teams hoisting trophies, a poster for last year's Christmas pantomime presented by the Amateur Drama

Society (The Twins, of course, are key members, there's a tiny picture of them in the corner, dressed as festive flower pots) and a photo gallery of last month's fundraising walk round the lake.

Songstress Gloria Gaynor is ranting from the loudspeakers, forecasting her survival. I know it's time for me to turn around and face the crowd. I turn, lean back against the notice board. Shite move, what if someone wants to read notices. Too late. I Will Survive.

I tap out the beat as if I get it. I catch the eye of someone in my class, the one with the Bird's-Eye Views project from last summer. She looks away so I do too, like talking to her was the last thing I'd want. Then I'm whistling along, the stupidest thing ever as now the song is beginning to end. I decide I'll wait until the next song starts and then I'll nip into the ladies' jacks, just get a breather, get a hold of myself, what the hell am I so het up about? What the hell do I care about this bunch of shitehawks? Oh no not I. Crowd of saps the lot of them, as my brother said before he left for Melbourne last September.

<u>Things To Do When You Don't Know What To Do</u>

- Tie your shoelaces (untie them first)
- Work at an imaginary stain on your sleeve

- Fold one arm over your belly and bring the other to your face, tapping your cheekbone to mimic deep thought (not too fast or you'll look demented)
- Have a pretend conversation with someone in the distance, use hand gestures but avoid dramatic moves (be very cautious, this can backfire)
- If you're smart enough to be carrying a notepad and pen (bring one with you whenever you leave your house), list things on it

There's a crackling over the loudspeakers, the next song is coming. I'm all set to take off into the ladies' as soon as the music swings into action. First come the trumpets and, next thing you know, the hall is thick with the sound of the Village People's 'YMCA'. Everyone races to the dance floor. I start slinking off but somebody appears in front of me. An older boy, not local. I don't know him. He obviously doesn't know me.

He's asking me something. I say *what* in a screechy kind of way. He leans in, says *wanna dance* and I say *sure*, and he turns and walks onto the dance floor and I lope after him and then we're in the middle of the lot of them, swaying. I see

The Twins through the crowd and they're with two milky boys. Arms are flailing and everyone is shouting *Wye-Em-Sea-Ay!* and here is this boy, dancing beside me as if all of it is fine, and he's smiling and I start smiling because this is funny, this is good, and I'm moving along to the Village People and the coloured lights are whirling over everyone and I'm singing and when the chorus comes he starts the arms-as-letters thing and I try to copy him and haven't a clue but keep going at it anyway and I'm singing as loud as everyone else *Wye-Em-Sea-Ay!* and he reaches over and takes my arms and does the Y for me, does the M, the C, the A for me, his hands on my elbows, and I look around to see if The Twins are watching, me the same as everyone, me dancing with an older boy, we're singing, we're moving together, me doing the Y, the M, the C, the A, it's not that hard, I'm good at it, *it's fun to stay at the Wye-Em-Sea-Ay-Ay!*

And then, then, the music is starting to fade, the song is ending. Shite. What now.

The song has ended and I'm standing there looking at this boy who asked me, and people are leaving the dance floor and he seems to be hunching towards a leaving too because he takes a step away and I move to stay close to him because there are people walking in between us now because they're leaving because there's no music and I tap my foot as if to some secret beat just to keep the good thing going because he's looking to his friends and it seems to me the boy doesn't know what to do, but I do, and there's nobody on the floor now except me and him and the coloured lights swirling and I say *what's your name* and he doesn't answer, just keeps looking back to his friends who are laughing, is it at us, at me. The loudspeaker crackle starts up again. Another song. And I do know why he doesn't answer. But I'm just thinking: *maybe.*

The sound of shivery flute rises, like a ghost is on its way. Couples come onto the dance floor. It's 'Bright Eyes' by Garfunkel, it's the Slow Set. Me and this boy, we're still standing together on the edge of the floor, standing where we don't belong because the Slow Set is for couples only. The real ones are starting to dance around us like zombies. I reach my hand up to touch his shoulder. He turns, says *thank you* and leaves.

I'm standing on the edge, half-in, half-out, my hand still held up. I shove it deep into my pocket, my brother's jeans pocket, why did I wear these, what the feck is wrong with me, no cop. I feel the pebbles, and my compass. I close my fingers around it. These stupid trousers are too big for me. I look down at the floor. The coloured lights are weaving east and west, north and south, marking figure eights on the floorboards.

<u>Things I Should Have Done Instead of What I Did</u>

- Legged it off the dance floor the moment YMCA was spelt out for the last time, saying 'thank-you-good-night' to the boy
- Replied: 'To this shite? Not in a trillion light years' when he asked me to dance in the first place
- Headed straight for the ladies' jacks the minute I arrived, and stayed there, counting the dead moths
- Remained in the Cortina and told The Wally to drive me around if he likes driving that much
- Stayed in my room

I hear the sneering begin. Some of the couples have started to bump into me for the laugh, saying *oops a speed bump*. And here's Garfunkel chanting away, what is it, a glorious death-river to be followed downstream by those with cop, it appears. Deep breath is what Mam always suggests when things go black. I get the idea of what to do. She'd be disappointed. Sorry, Mam.

I think of my room, just six fields, a wood and one slow stream away. My room, not much more than a half-hour trek from here, as the crow flies. My good thing south-west of where I'm currently standing among these gits. I shove hard the next couple who bash into me. They skittle into another couple. The lot of them give me wide berth then, gawking at me standing there with the compass in my hand.

Look, yes, the fire is lit, I have it hot-strong in my head. I'm thinking about the bees, how they dance for each other, to tell each other the fastest way to a good thing nearby, nectar for the babies, nectar for the queen. I check the compass, and turn to face south-west. I picture a figure-of-eight pattern on the floor, put myself in the eight's centre, twirl once for the crowd like the ballerina in my old wind-up music box, and start to do the bees' Waggle Dance. March forward leftwise, quivering like a belly dancer, two, three, four steps, a wide turn to the right, circle back to the starting point, one foot in front of the other, no one says a word other than Garfunkel's keening about eyes on fire, another waggle run forward, two, three, four steps, turn to the left, back to the starting point and forward again, a jittering spectacular is I, six fields, a wood, a stream is what I'm saying, it's not far, go.

I'm thinking of The Twins (forward shudder) their eyes (turn to the right) somewhere out there (circle back). And now I feel tears rising, my fire dousing. I do one more run-through. When the final circuit is nearly finished, I ready myself. Don't stall, don't look around. Go. I run in the direction of the door. Some start to clap. I push through the crowd and it parts, closing in after me like a zipper. I leave, into the night air, the door swings shut behind.

The Wally is already parked up, waiting, leaning against the bonnet, practising his smoke rings. He doesn't see me. I give the two fingers to his back, slow and special for him, then say loud *Well fancy meeting you here, Big Wally*. When he turns, I tell him I think he's a brilliant driver. *Really?* he says, *you messing or what?* He opens the passenger door. I blow him a kiss. *Must dash*, I say.

I skirt around the back of the building. I hear him calling after me. I run into the dark, up over the ditch, across the night fields, towards my wood, my cold little stream, and I know now what this summer's school project's going to be, it's going to be about the sword razor shells I found in the woods, them so very far from shore, and all the possible reasons how they got to be in that particular place among the trees many many miles from where they belong.

GOLDEN STONE TERRITORY

It's early evening, after the last feed of the day. She's meandering through a garden thick with hoverflies and scents. She pauses frequently, gathering pockets of information, some new, some old, some ancient, cross-referencing each with her memories of the same journey this time yesterday. Her path appears chaotic: forward, reverse, a tight circle, stall, forward. She only knows what she's looking for when she finds it. Pausing, she analyses each find before moving on towards the next.

Nose down, the tips of the grass catch the diamanté *B* that tinkles from her collar. She finds a place where another bitch has urinated. The mark wasn't there yesterday. Snorting the scent, she notes: unfamiliar, close to oestrus, well-fed, a recent trespass. Manoeuvring her rump over the spot, she urinates in short robust spurts, and pads on.

She's making for the rear of the house. Though her snout skims the ground, her ears are cocked for sound. Usually the old man has appeared at the door at this point, roaring in her direction and striking the doorstep with his stick. She always slinks away from this challenge, her ghost tail held between her legs (it was docked at birth but she does not know this), heading back towards the scraggy hole she made in the privet hedge separating her home territory from this no-man's-land compilation of scents.

Yesterday, on her way back home through the hedge, she sniffed out a mystery: her own faeces, which she'd excreted earlier in no-man's-land, now wrapped in a small plastic bag, hanging caught on her side of the hedge, the scent of her excrement paired with the scent of the old man.

Sometimes there is commotion, an exciting hostility, when he flings stones from the driveway at her as she retreats. She chases down these trophies in the grass. This seems to make him even more aggressive. The game, if the man plays it, is this: he shouts and throws, she catches and runs for escape, muzzle aloft, holding the prized golden stone stamped with the thrilling smell of her human territorial rival. Back home, she deposits these trophies among her collection of sticks and stones by her own back door, gifts for her pack.

This evening, there's no man. She gives this little consideration, dealing only with what there is, being incapable of dealing with what there is not. Reaching the top of the garden, she defecates, and paws clumps of soft lawn over her excrement before moving nervously onto the golden gravel of the driveway, in front of the old man's door.

Here, among the small pebbles, she detects a series of unfamiliar scents. All human. One female, two males. Adults. Not the man from the front door. Latticed around these humans are curious traces of agitation. She notes the scents but does not linger, having edged onto what is undeniably the old man's territory. Heading for the rear, a place where territorial rights are still in dispute, she trots across the gravel and skirts past the side of the house. Poking her head around the back corner, she spots the cat's bowl.

The cat is sitting on the threshold at the back door, staring at her, having discerned her approach long before. He flattens his ears, swings his tail, but both know this is no contest. She ignores the faint feline hiss and pads up to his bowl, barely noticing the cat jumping away with a grousing flourish. She gnaws at the remains of the cat food; there are some dried bits left clinging to the sides but no tinge of morning-milk remnant. She's about to investigate the yielding hatch of the compost bin when she senses the cat engaging. He's sitting now inside the threshold, enveloped in the safety of the man's interior terrain. His tail curls contentment around neat paws. He jeers at her through the open back door.

This is new. There is a wide-open door. There is no old man, no stick, no shouting, no game in motion. The two animals lock stares. The cat streaks inward. She follows him, hopping over the conceded threshold, entering the house.

The old man's domain is dark. She draws in layered indications of him. Other unsettling scents linger from the recent past; on the walls, the floor, the stairs. The kitchen door is agape, the room is empty of life. She walks in.

The combined essence of the three humans she identified earlier is here, vestiges of adrenaline edged with less tangible elements of panic. She pads over the broken crockery and sniffs at the upturned drawers and overturned chairs. No immediate edibles here, though she can ascertain the possibility of food behind the strewn sachets of granulated soup and boxes of dried marrowfat peas on the floor.

An intimation of cat floats in. Turning to find the source, she sees him crouching on the stairs, glaring at her through the banisters. His pupils are wide with alarm. Whiskers lifting, he starts to hiss again. His anxiety excites her. She yips, running straight at him. He flees hissing up the stairs. She chases, her high-pitched yelping resounding off the walls as she scales the steps in giant little leaps.

She stops on the landing. The scents here frighten. The old man: present. Blood: his. Urine: his. Blended undertones of fear, of injury, relics of a troubling wound. Several doors are open. She enters the room that contains the source.

She cowers. Here is the old man. He's sitting slumped on a chair pulled up to an iron-frame bed. His torso is tied to the chair, his arms are tied behind him and bound to the bed frame with reams of duct tape. The tape covers his mouth, torn strips running around his head. Blood-stained mucus trickles from his nose, over the tape, tracking through a stubbly chin before dripping onto the old floral carpet. His eyes are open, he's looking towards the door, towards her.

She determines he is immobile, no immediate threat. She sits and observes him. He snorts, but there's no challenge in the tone, just pain, exhaustion, dehydration, a fragment of anticipation.

She looks away, registers the cat perched on top of the wardrobe. He begins to emit a low grumbling whirr, gawping down at her.

The iron bed is against the wall, by the window. A mottled shaving mirror on the bedroom's old mantelpiece reflects the setting sun slicing in through the window's half-drawn curtains. The bedside drawers have been toppled, their contents scattered. Papers, glasses, a blue-crowned bottle of Lourdes holy water, pens, photographs, cufflinks tied with fishing line, a comb. Nothing menacing here. She turns her head to scissor-itch her hindquarters, paws scratching purchase on the carpet.

Blinking dried blood from his eyelids, the old man starts to moan. After a struggle, he arranges the gurgling sound into a sing-song incantation, raising the pitch at the end of each bar. She knows this is directed at her. Without turning her head from her rump, she listens, considering the nuances of his tone. Suddenly recognizing the inflection as an invite to play, she replies with an excited yelp and jumps up, docked tail wagging. Pelt-stiff, the cat crescents.

Trouser-leg sodden with urine, the man taps his foot on the carpet. She runs to the spot, whimpering with delight, scratching furious where he has indicated. He moves his foot and taps a different place. She jumps to the new indication, looks up at him, anticipating. She knows this type of game, she plays it at home.

Stretching his foot forwards, he taps the holy-water bottle. She yelps, runs to it, grabs it in her mouth, runs to the door, runs back, whirls several elated tight circles in front of him, drops it at his feet, yelping a cracked full stop. She waits, tongue lolling, gazing back and forth from his face to his feet, her little barrel chest surging.

He turns his head slowly, looking around the darkening room. Small whines rise from his lungs. The distress she discerns in him confuses her. She draws in her tongue, cocks her head.

His eyes come to rest on a colourful mantelpiece ornament propped beside his shaving mirror. The ceramic figurine depicts a jolly, ruddy-cheeked, balding man brandishing a fishing rod. The engraving on the base reads: *To Desmond on your Retirement Best Wishes from your Neighbours Nora & Gerard (& your pal Bantam!)*

He slides his torso down the chair as low as his ties will allow. Pelvis perched on the edge, he stretches out his leg towards the fireplace. She observes, eagerly following the foot's progress.

The man's foot travels up the fire-surround and reaches the edge of the mantelpiece. The figurine is pushed back against the wall. He positions his foot in front of it, taps, stops, taps again, intoning with a series of high-pitched little whines from behind his gag the sing-song invitation to play.

She has watched his foot's journey, has deciphered what's expected of her. She jumps. Her muzzle tips the edge of the mantelpiece, she falls back down. Pushing onto her squat haunches, she jumps again, higher, angling her head in towards the ceramic figurine. She grabs at it. She has it. She celebrates in frenzied twirls, yelping through clamped jaws, then drops the prize at his feet.

He pulls himself back into an upright sitting position, wincing behind his spittle-filled gag. Bringing his foot over the dropped figurine, the man hovers there, bolstering Bantam's attention. Ears raised, she whines in expectation. He taps on it. She snatches it up into her mouth, runs to the door, runs back to him, circles his legs, runs to the door, runs back, drops it once more at his feet.

He taps again, she grabs it again, getting a firm grip, familiar now with the game. She runs in spinning twirls towards the door, the figurine held tight in her jaws, her nose tipping her tail-stump. Round and round she chases herself, delaying the drop at his feet to draw out the thrill.

As she spins, he raises his leg high, pauses, brings it crashing down onto the floor. The powerful thump shocks her. She stops short, figurine still gripped. Stares at him. This is not the game.

He inhales fast through blocked nostrils, and lets out as loud as sharp a shriek as he can through his gag. Atop the wardrobe, the cat begins to bawl, ears flat as blades. The man starts to wriggle, violently, shaking the chair. Cold fear rising in her, she continues to stare. He bashes his foot hard off the floor once more, then kicks out repeatedly at the iron legs of his bed, the sounds clamouring against the walls.

She flees, ghost-tail held tight between her legs, the terror-howls of man and cat chasing her. She bolts down the stairs, out the back door, across his golden stones, heading straight for the privet portal, the figurine trophy with his name emblazoned on it still held in her strong little terrier jaws, back to her own territory, back to her own pack who'll be waiting for her, wondering where she's been, wondering why there are no lights on next door, none for these past two nights, at least.

THE SUNDIAL PILGRIMAGE

It's morning. I'm off again to my tree, my bundle of tricks slung over my shoulder, the summer solstice having played out a few weeks ago.

Every year since the event, when summer is beginning to close in, I go to a different part of the vast forest. There, I select a tree. I always have difficulty choosing. Last year I did a young silver birch, its leaves still sapping green. It took me until early autumn, tangled up in the filigree of lean branches from dawn to dark. The little heart-shaped leaves were difficult to work. My fingers were pricked red-raw, my old eyes gone askew. But all these leaves deserve a chance, and for as long as I'm standing I'm not giving up on a single one.

This summer, I've headed east. I found a spindly rowan tree, old enough to have proved its viability and young enough to warrant my help. Rowan leaves are fragile, rowans fancy themselves as strapping ash but in truth they're nothing like that. The delicate leaflets are arranged around a stem, about twenty to each, though every baby thinks it's the only one.

I set to, selecting a slender needle from my bag. With it, I choose a silk thread, blue in contrast to the leaf's green in order to map my progress as I work. I've learnt that one unbroken thread-length is best for use on all leaflets radiating from the central stem. Doubling it up and releasing as I sew. A tiny knot at the end. I place the initial snick cautiously, beside a minuscule vein for strength and some ballast for my knot. I start at the terminal leaf, gently piercing the fine-grained cuticle.

The first leaf is always challenging. Sometimes I ask whether it feels pain, any panic in the young tree it's clinging to, sap fizzing, does it understand the struggle ahead, the stealthy magnet below. Sometimes, when I sense fear from the leafling, I sing a lullaby.

Centred between apex, petiole and midrib, I pull the thread through. When there's a neat line of stitches perforating the leaf side to side, I sew down towards where the leaf grasps the axis, weaving the thread with the blade's vascular network. On reaching the base, I circle it, trussing the embroidered leaflet to its stem. I pull the thread taut, without strangling the living anchor, then stitch my way back up the adjoining leaflet in an unbroken track of blue filament.

I know I'm being overly specific, too intricate, but I don't know which detail could reasonably be left out and which is integral to the structure, a joist, girder, a load-bearing beam. Even if I wanted to, it's impossible for me now to revert to succinct, to detached abstractions, impossible after everything that has happened.

I work through each glossy blade, fastening them to the stem. I'm careful not to tear the tender green lamina or angle any leaf away from the sky. Each one of them has a predestined position on the stem which I don't entitle myself to interfere with, my parameters rigidly set from the beginning. To follow the rules without enquiry is the strongest tool in my tricks-bag. Ready, wily as a weasel, I sew.

Once each leaflet is tied, I wind the thread around the main stem, binding down to where it attaches to the twig and circling there, the blue distinct against the duskiness of the bark. With little left of the thread, I loosen the last few swirls around the twig and run it in under. I pull to confirm that it has bound, that the coming weeks of residual growth will ensure the thread becomes embedded in the tree's flesh. Thus the little rowan leaf is rendered safe. Gravity will have no say here.

It is trying work. It'll take many more weeks to finish just this one young tree. Each stem bears several hopeful leaflets, each twig several stems, each secondary branch several twigs, and the trunk is host to a multitude of lanky juvenile branches brightly reaching skyward, away from the middle, the attachments becoming weaker and more vulnerable the further from the roots.

But the dark matriarchs. The patriarchs. The ancient towerers at the centre of the forest. Those trees whose thick branches attach directly to the trunk have resolve. They will bend for no bloodsucking younger branches, no transient fruit, no storm. Nor will they bend for any howl, any terrible prayer screamed directly into their bole, any yearn tugging at their rooted strength. A lonely hawthorn on a mountaintop learns to bow to the prevailing wind but the trees at the core of the forest have no such humility.

The towerer at the dark middle of the forest. She's still alive, I can feel it, in the soil, her roots entangled with all the others. I orbit around the edges, but never will I go deep in there again. I won't breathe its loamy air, I won't walk its profane ground. As slight as I am, as feeble, I still have my will. I have resolve.

On that day, the day of the event, I was walking, there, close to the centre, through waning bluebells, light-hearted. It was my everyday walk, at midday, away from home. Away from my sit-stand desk, my laptop. The selection of fine-nibbed pencils, the rolls of architectural tracing paper. Away from my first-draft sketches and into the old forest, to arrange thoughts, to arrange the day's plan for a sequence of rough designs for the council's proposed refugee centre on the outskirts of the city. The city I lived in, contentedly, for the duration of my marriage. The city and marriage I'd left for a small holding, an old cottage backed up to the forest, its now-overgrown garden spilling freely into where the two tenderly touch.

The event. It was late spring, all peace among the trees. I was head in the clouds, lines swirling, atriums, balustrades, cantilevers. I heard something, not trees, not leaves nor roots nor animals. I didn't know. I heard something coming from the centre. How could I have known. I went closer, got down on my hunkers in the veiny undergrowth, limbs folded like a hare.

A man, there, in a clearing, maybe ten yards from where I crouched among the fading bluebells and bloodless leaves. A young man, alone. Clean-shaven, a jacket too big for his shoulders, boots too big for his feet. Ox-blood boots, labourer's boots. A man, way in among the towerers at the centre of this tangle of forest.

He was gathering fallen branches from around the base of an ancient ash tree, piling them together to construct what resembled a poor man's pyre. He was arranging these half-rotten branches underneath a stout bough which forked repeatedly as it diverged outward and upward from its huge mother-trunk. Occasionally, he stepped onto the structure, jumping lightly. The weaker branches cracked under him and he jumped harder, pressing the splintered down. He continued the primitive construction, checking its strength every now and then, and yes, I had cause to wonder. Solid cause to wonder. But I stayed rooted, noting each specific structural detail, every small engineering decision, too stupid to turn my head and walk away, to slink away weightless, to forget about it all.

When he had the wooden pyre high enough, the top mess of branches raised up by the compressed detritus beneath, he stood on it once more. This time, it remained firm, hoisting him a yard or so above the ground. I watched him reach inside his jacket and remove a thick hemp rope. He looked to the bough above him. Holding one end of the cording, a crude knot tying a circle together, he swung the other end skyward. It whistled around the bough and fell back to him. Knees bent to lower his stature by about a head's height, he hoisted until the noose hung as halo just above. He swirled the loose end several more times around the bough, pulling it taut. He gripped the rope in one hand and the noose in the other. Lifting himself up, he tested the overhanging bough by imposing his full weight. The rope moaned, but the bough remained unmoved.

And still there I stayed, watching it all.

He climbed off his scaffold. He tugged at the rope and, confident it had found steady purchase, wound the remainder about the trunk, tying it. He returned to his rickety mound of dead wood and climbed back up, arms held cruciform for balance, mindful this time not to snap any of the remaining branches. Standing to full height, he brought his legs together and took some time to find equilibrium, shifting his ox-blood boots, making small adjustments. From where I watched, the braided noose surrounded his pale young face like a Victorian locket.

He looked once more at the bough. Then he stilled, hands clasped in front of his crotch. I recall he cleared his throat.

Imagine that. Imagine remembering that. The sound was bare, wispy.

He took the noose, slipped it over his head.

And still, there I lay, watching the whole thing like it was mine.

He tightened it, the ignorant knot fisted at his ear, and he sighed, a slow exhalation, guillotined at the end with the snap of a small cough. He leapt in the air and on his descent scissor-kicked the pyre of sticks beneath. They scattered, leaving him swinging wild. His hands flew straight to his neck, clawing at the rope. The sound he made was a fractured, a crackling kind of whir, I hear it still. His legs continued to lash out, but, with nothing left to strike, they danced a hopeless savagery. One boot flew off, landing in front of me. Its ox-blood tongue lolled. A roar at last sprang from my throat.

I ran to him, grasped his thrashing legs, heaved him up as best I could above my shoulders. His heels dug into my belly, his crackling spat down on me. I tried to hold him, putting myself between him and Earth's central magnet. But I am slight, there never was much to me.

His balance shifted, veering left, right. Cursing the drag reaching up from the ground, I tried to correct my stance, but the more I moved the more he spun, this way, that. My arms were weakening. After a time, a duration I still cannot settle on, I howled at him that I couldn't hold him much longer, it was futile, I was sorry, so sorry for everything. I sang out the sorry like a prayer, trying to hush his fear. Soon the Earth's pull broke my grip and I fell face down onto the remains of his scaffold.

Lying there, I started up my song again, this time trying to null his presence above me. But I could hear him. I ventured to look up. He was still kicking, weakly, the white sock on his bootless foot twirling like a child's flag. His hands clutched at the embedded rope, nails feebly scratching into his neck. I found his eyes, they were wholly present. I shouted to him to give up, stop, there was nothing more either of us could change. I turned away, readying myself to run. But as soon as my eyes left his, I knew what I had to do.

I gathered what strengths I had, channelling them all into my limbs. I leapt high in the air and threw my arms vice-like around his thighs, my legs tight around his calves, binding myself to him, arresting his spasms. And there I hung, gripping him monkey-like, adding my parasitic weight to his, further bait for the magnet below. Yes, he tried to rid himself of me, fingernails hooking strands of my hair, body writhing to lose my fatal mass. Ineffectual. I had resolve.

Thus coupled, we swung like a pendulum, back and forth, back and forth, ticking off each miserable second, each minute. My commitment to him was unbreakable, I hope he knew. Perched cross-legged on his feet, I sang him a lullaby. In between each sugary verse, I shushed, and felt his suffering fade as I delivered him to his end.

Over time, a long, unspeakable time, our pendulum unwound to a stop. In the descending silence at the core of the forest, I turned my face up. Black blood had congealed around my companion's nostrils, spittle dropping from a slack mouth. He was gone. At last, this young man in oversized wear was gone.

I retrieved his missing ox-blood boot and placed it back on him, first restoring the sock still dangling from his foot. I tied the laces, securing them neatly with a double knot. I did the same to the other boot, unfastening then refastening to match. Finally, turning my back on the young man, the rope, the bough, the tree, the dark ground in the middle of the forest, I walked away.

With each step, the Earth sucked at my soles, pooling their blood. Though my gaze was forward, I could hear the low crackle of his bough behind me, the sigh of the rope, the drips of his spittle counting out my steps as I left him alone, as alone and uncoupled as I was, turning slowly on a knot.

I did not go home to my desk and the laptop and the vellum and the cardboard mock-up of a multi-storied glass-fronted butterfly-roofed building with a series of tiny grey nuclear families looking inward and outward at each other. Skirting the edge of the forest, I walked for miles, for days, everything inside me re-arranging. I hid at night, finding low bushes to crease into. I was held wakeful by visions of his suspended figure, an inept sundial at the centre of the wreathing forest. I pictured his spine stretched straight as a zealous sapling. I pictured him shrouded by the web of branches, destined never to count out with circling shadow the hours, the years.

Several black days later, when I'd gathered my thoughts, I returned in darkness to my house, cautious as an intruder. I was there only to gather the makings of a shelter: a tarpaulin, groundsheet, blankets, matches, traps that I'd inherited with the house. And my bag of tricks, to begin this undertaking, the needlework project I'd blueprinted over those days of treading the forest. Before leaving, I unplugged the laptop and disconnected the house from the internet, from any communications satelliting above. I returned to the forest through the back door.

My visits home are rare. My old garden has become indistinguishable from the forest it lies up against. Just once, I stayed overnight, to record these events, to chart them as clearly as I could, standing at my desk, protractor, T-square, compass. I entered my bedroom, observed myself in the mirror. Cheekbones, iliac crests of my hip bone, all else dark and dirt. My clothes threadbare. My resolve. I slept curled by the open back door, nose to knee, listening, ready to bolt like a fox back into the forest at the slightest indication of my own species, their sound, their acrid smell, their questions.

The late-summer night is closing in, the moon is beginning to glow through a lattice of leaves. I'm sitting in the heart of my rowan. Every leaf to the right of me I have sewn good and tight to its branchling. Those to the left I have yet to address. It will take many more weeks to finish this one. The sutures on the secured catch the moonlight, the thread-tracks forming a miniature city. The leaflets that remain unstitched flitter like cornered moths, waiting, some losing their grip and falling. I know I cannot help them all.

Later tonight, I'll climb down. I'll lie beneath my tarpaulin, atop the ground some distance away, against this unholy magnet, feeling its persistent drag downward through my throat, my lungs, my womb. Bats, badgers, pine martens active around me, all of us feeling the spool winding. My eyes will close on the embers of my campfire, pulp of dandelion roots and sweet flag I roasted earlier tracking through my guts. I won't rise until I smell the summer dawn. And when it blinks through the leaves remaining, I'll search out sustenance. A tender rabbit caught in my trap, a horde of glistening snails clustered on yesterday's detritus, a fistful of watercress, a sip from a cold limestone spring. Then, belly full, I'll resume my needlework.

JONQUILLE

There is a young woman, wrong, there is not. She's not yet an adult, but she's not still a child. She's in her teens. She wants to be considered an adult, let it be she's accorded that. Begin again.

There is a young adult sitting beneath a tree. She may be carrying a viable embryo inside her, she may not be.

What's to be said about the tree? Well, first, this is no wind-shook sapling. It's immense. Unlike the changeling who sits cross-legged on the damp evening ground, the tree is fully grown. It's a lone, cold-blooded, straight-grained ash tree in the middle of a field. At the first autumnal winds, it'll shed its leaves, easily and without thought, even while they're still working green.

But, for now, for this late spring dusk, its new leaves shimmer unhindered, twisting hopeful towards the day's last inkling of light. For now, its dark roots bury, visible for only a short space above ground before disappearing down into the earth.

And what's to be said about this earth? Little can be said with certainty about the ground underfoot. Roots bury, invisible things, et cetera.

It's a Sunday, twilight. She sits, cross-legged, leaning against the tree, hands on her knees. Eight of her nails are varnished blue-grey, the middle two a lustrous yellow. She has a silver stud in one eyebrow and a tattoo of a crimson heart behind her left ear.

Her tattoo is recent; she had to wait for her seventeenth birthday. The bedroom mirror has confirmed what her best friend tells her: the heart is slightly skewed, the lines don't quite join up, its blood-red appears to be constantly on the verge of spilling out. But there it is, imperfect, behind her left ear.

Jonquille is the name she did not read on the nail-varnish bottle when she blindly pulled it out of her cosmetics drawer earlier this afternoon, before things began to unfold. Had she read the name, she would by now have decided there was some magical implication to the coincidence of her later striding through a field of daffodils to get here, to her tree, striding through a lush field of *Narcissus jonquilla* bobbing and bowing around her as she tipped their yellow flower heads with her fingers. But she has not read the name on the varnish bottle, therefore hasn't had any thoughts on coincidences and mysterious happenings, and whether or not anything can ever be really described as an accident.

This afternoon, before pulling out the tear-shaped bottle whose name she didn't read, she had first varnished her nails with her favourite: a pearlescent blue-grey named Misty Dawn. After it dried, she'd closed her eyes, stuck her hand back into the drawer, shuffled the little glass containers and drew out a bright yellow bottle, an as-yet-unopened birthday present from her best friend ('because of "Yellow Flicker Beat"' her friend had said as she handed it to her at her birthday party several Saturdays ago in TGI Friday's and, arms locked in the leatherette booth, they'd sung the song together, *I'm a princess cut from marble, smoother than a storm, and the scars that mark my body, they're silver and gold*).

The new yellow varnish in hand, she'd closed the drawer with a nudge of her hip, sat on the edge of the bed, and thought of that day, of that night, her seventeenth birthday party, what she wore, what she looked like, what she hoped she looked like to others. Conjuring a plausible image of what her birthday-self might have looked like, she varnished her two ring fingers, the rich golden yellow glossed over the pearlescent blue-grey underneath.

She always painted her nails this way; first, all of the fingers in her trusty Misty Dawn and, second, just the two ring fingers in whatever colour the universe decreed, which today had been yellow. And also today, after the nails, she was going to undertake the other business, what she needed to do but hadn't yet, but was going to, soon, after the nails were sorted, after the universe was consulted and everything was clear and calm. (Later, while walking through the daffodils to her ash tree, clutching the test-stick in one hand and tipping the flower heads with her other, she wasn't thinking about fingernails and this is the reason any potential significance regarding the apparent randomness of colour choice, the yellow, and now, here, the daffodils, did not materialize.)

Let this ash be described as faithful. This is how she perceives it. It has endured alone in the centre of this field and is likely to endure for some time to come. Because she can see it from her bedroom window, and has been noting its seasonal changes since she first became aware of seasonal and cyclical changes, she considers it hers, imagines there's a connection, an unspoken understanding between them. This could be why she has chosen to sit beneath it this evening surrounded by its fallen winged fruit, could be why she sits pelvis to ground, spine to bark. This possible reason, but if so, not this alone. The tree will endure with or without her, above and below the ground, mostly below. The other reason is that here beneath the tree is not home. It's close enough to home but cannot be confused with home despite being so near she could possibly be seen, and maybe summoned, if that Sunday evening unlikelihood was a want.

What's to be said about home? This: she's decided that beneath her ash is the only place to make the call. (No, it's too soon to mention the call. She's not ready. She sits under the tree, that's enough.)

She has cleared her throat, many times. It has begun to hurt. She clears her throat to overcome the fear.

She listens to herself clearing her throat but nothing's clear and nothing's clearing. The tree's not working, the ground's not working.

She looks at her two yellow nails, brings them side by side, contemplates which one looks best. One nail is sealed perfectly, the lacquer extending in a glossy stripe from nail bed to tip. The second stripe finishes in a translucent blur; she can see right through to the Misty Dawn beneath. Why are these two nails not the same? Was it not her intention to have them the exact same? It was. Sometimes things just happen.

She clicks her nails together, clears her throat again. Looks to home. Nobody at the kitchen window. What does it matter? Nobody at the upstairs bedroom windows. What does any of it matter? Looks to see if she has closed the back door behind her. She knows she has closed the door, but the knowing doesn't make anything clear.

She checks if she could be spotted from any of the windows. She's already sure there's no one in the kitchen, no one in the bedrooms. Her parents and younger siblings are still in the sitting room at the front of the house; she'd sat among them before walking to the tree. They're watching a pre-watershed disaster film on Sky. She told them she's going to her room, she'd seen this film before.

She shimmies left, around the trunk. She's out of sight. She pulls her knees to her chest, turns her feet in. Let the branch network overhead metaphor into some kind of umbrella; shield-like, it could be said, but allowing occasional blinks of light to tweak through. The sun is setting, tiny shards appear and disappear around her. The knotted ground circling the trunk is dry, it has felt little rain in years.

Taking out her phone, she checks the coverage, the charge. She knows there's coverage; this is her tree, this is her call place. She knows her phone is charged, she didn't leave home until it was 85 per cent. She left home headed in a straight line for her ash, primed to be an adult.

The phone has dropped to 82 per cent. She thinks of the charge draining through her hand, spine, into the trunk, down to the roots, beyond, going where? searching anchorage underground maybe, embed there, in the dark, some sort of footing is it. She doesn't know where the charge goes. Tiny things burying, is what she's thinking about. A thing that wants to be considered good. She feels a cocooned panic fluttering inside her. A countdown. Is it a want. What is it, if it is not a want.

Tapping one yellow nail off the screen, she looks at a photo, a close-up of herself and a young man, an attractive young man. He's one year older than her, he'd like to be considered a man, and would expect to be described as attractive.

The photo is from her birthday party. Wherever he is now, he doesn't know he's smiling at her in her phone. It's a selfie, she was facing the camera when she took it. She looks at herself looking back, she looks at him smiling at the other her.

She turns her face up towards the ash leaves. They're stirring, a breeze is sifting through them. There are two things to think about: the party in TGI Friday's, and after.

She sees the dark of his body forming, him saying her name, remembers the clearness of it coming from his mouth, his silver necklace, no, his hemp necklace with a silver pendant, braided brown hemp, silver St Brigid's cross, cold, falling on her face, him saying her name to the imperfect crimson heart behind her ear. The rustle of the ash leaves now binds with her memory of these things.

Grips the phone to steer this good from draining.

Sits up straight, clears her throat, goes to Contacts, taps his name.

His avatar surfaces, his name in italics beneath.

She taps Call.

She's spelt his name with an '*i*' instead of a '*y*'. The phone's ringing. She's not sure if she should've spelt it with an '*i*' or a '*y*'. She's not sure if he was smiling at her or at something else, something behind her, a thing beyond, a thing she doesn't know. The phone's ringing. Should it be an '*i*' or a '*y*'. She's not sure. Is he smiling in the photo. The phone's ringing, it's possible he's not smiling, she doesn't know, it's possible she spelt his name wrong, it's possible he wasn't looking at her, the phone's ringing, it could be this isn't his number or she dialled wrong, did he give her a wrong number, did she dial incorrectly the wrong number he gave her, a woman answers, this is his mam he'll kill me for answering his phone hold on he's up in his bedroom on the PS5 as usual ha ha d'ya want to hold on for a moment please thanks he'll be delighted hold on there sweetie okay.

She waits, touching the small stick in her pocket, a flat plastic stick branded with two blue lines in a little window at its tip. A tiny message, beginning in the window on the tip of the stick in her pocket.

In the packaging, there were instructions on how to read these stripes. The instruction leaflet lies read and re-read on top of the unread bottle of Jonquille at the bottom of her cosmetics drawer in her bedroom. *Note: during the early stages of the first trimester, the possibility of miscarriage is at its highest.*

She leans into the tree, waiting.

There is an ending in sight. If there now was an image presented of her crying, it's likely any tears tendered would be made to slide fast down her face and vanish into the dry ground, ground that's been sheltered for decades by the umbrella of branches overhead. In such a scenario, the ground would disappear those few tears as if it's nothing to take them on, as if its vastness makes it insatiable.

So, what's to be said about this ending? First, she's not crying. Here she is, waiting. She's biting her lip and shuffling the ash's winged fruit with her feet. His avatar is pressed to her ear, close to the skewed heart. Let her yellow nails bury into her palms. The phone's screen will darken by default after ten seconds.

He gets to her within seven. Hi, he says, hi was hoping you'd call wasn't sure should I call or what where are you, are you at your tree.

SEBASTIAN

None of us had ever heard a name like it before. The lads have all quit their football games in the school playground since he arrived last month; instead they stand around during break time, whispering to Sebastian about The Project this The Project that. No slagging, real serious, like as if it was some kind of secret warfare.

The Project means deciding who Sebastian is going to chase around the playground today. Usually, it's one of us girls. He chased both of The Twins together one day because they never leave each other's side. Sometimes, he chases one of the boys who don't bother with football, the boys who prefer to hang around the swings and the monkey bars. Never the Travellers, they'd clock you if you tried anything funny.

He's standing in the middle of of the pile of football lads, nodding, his hair gelled lovely, his arms folded like he couldn't care less what they're saying, like he already knows himself what he's going to do and they're all just bores he puts up with in case they're useful, which is something I know something about.

I'm not looking for Sebastian to chase me, I'm not even thinking of who's left that he hasn't chased yet, or whether I might be next in the running, or not. But anyway. The other thing to consider is, I'm the best sprinter in school. Well, the best if you don't count your wan Gráinne. She has those swish runners with stripes all over them. Except on the soles, I don't think they're there but I'm not sure because I never seen those soles, not up close, never got near enough to them, and not for the want of trying. Always just flashes of them running ahead of me at the community games each year. But, look it. For now, I'm second best, at least there's that.

I take a quick peek over to where he's standing, beyond, with the football lads around him as if they own him, which they don't, even though they think they do. He doesn't look like he's looking this direction. The non-football lads are on the monkey bars as usual, ignoring everyone, talking about important stuff.

The girls spot me looking and they says what are you gawking at him for, are you thinking about kissing him, do you fancy him or something, do you like his hair is it, are you thinking about him chasing you, do yous want to get married or what? And I tell them he can chase all he likes but there's no way he'll catch me and of course I don't fancy him but don't I have to watch out because wasn't I one of the wans not yet caught and mightn't he decide to try and catch me today so he might. And there was no way that was going to happen on account of my being at least the second-best sprinter, maybe the first best if I had the swish footwear, so, no, not happening, ladies, not today not ever.

That's more or less what I say to them. And they all start sniggering, and The Twins say I'm talking shite, and that makes me so flipping mad after all my careful explaining so I decide it's time to say something really really bad to Gráinne because that'll be sure to stop their sniggering, that'll be sure to cause a fuss.

Gráinne. She says it's from *grian*, the word for sun. I asked her once whether it might be from *gráin*, the word for *hate*, and she was not happy about that. Gráinne McGowan is the Best Sprinter in The School, according to the community games scoreboard in the classroom. Never defeated. Everyone round here is a bit afraid of her and all the girls want to be her best pal, or at least in her gang. The Twins are sort of like her assistants, reporting back to her about everything that goes on. She's the one that decides who's allowed be friends with who, the one who'll tell any of your secrets to anyone but you still better have a few secrets to tell her or she'll think you're being smart-arsed so the best thing to do is tell her something, anything, as long as it sounds private. She's the one who'll laugh at your lunch because you just have the soggy gooseberry jam sandwiches that your mam made but you can't flush them down the jacks because the Traveller kids have blocked the drains with throwing in the free buns they get because they don't care about buns and they don't care about trouble and the Travellers are the only ones Gráinne is afraid of because they don't care about her or her stripy runners.

So I turn to Gráinne, who's standing there with her fists on her hips all ready to have a good laugh about me looking over at Sebastian, and all the girls behind her saying that they seen me gawking over at him and why should Gráinne put up with a sneaky liar like me who thinks I'm better than her? And I says to her right there in front of everyone, 'Well,

I didn't see you sprinting away top speed yourself when he was chasing you yesterday, Gráinne, no, I didn't see you breaking your heart to get away from him with your big fat pink legs, now, did I, Gráinne? Ladies, I think this wan's gone soft on him!'

She goes pure wild at how I could say that as if I don't realize I'll be battered saying stuff like that about her and the others listening with their stupid mouths open and their eyes flittering between the two of us to see what'll happen next because something definitely has to happen after that.

She makes a grab for me, and with a raging head on her she roars 'Wedding bells for this wan! This wan wants to kiss him! This wan wants to marry Sebastian!' She drags me by the hair to the big fuchsia bush beside the field at the edge of the playground, with the swarm of girls running behind shouting 'Wedding bells! Wedding bells!' over at Sebastian, and The Twins saying things to Gráinne like 'That boy was so speedy, Gráinne! nobody blames you if you got caught by mistake!' talking like this as if they're the ones in trouble, as if they're the ones with a wad of hair caught in her hot fist and her dribbling crossways at having been shown up by the likes of me.

She shoves me down onto the muck under the old fuchsia, grabbing its droopy branches full of flowers and rain and swinging them over me. I stay dead still. I'm level with her runners and I can see now there's no stripes on them soles. I'm thinking, *don't get up, wait 'til she's gone, she doesn't matter*. The others are joining in, pulling at the poor old fuchsia and shouting 'Wedding bells, wedding bells' while its branches lash down their tiny red flowers on me like wet confetti. I've been through this type of craic before, I know it won't last long if I play-act like I'm scared. She'll soon quit and leave me be, drenched as I am with this muck and broken bits of fuchsia as if the birds shat berries all over me.

I hear a whistling, like some kind of signal. I look through the pack of girls to where Sebastian had been standing. And isn't he staring right back, hunched like a greyhound in the stall, set to make a run for me, and all the lads lined up behind him ready for The Project. I know what's coming next, what's happening at last, and I don't care about Gráinne nor the muck nor the banjaxed flowers all over me nor all the roaring girls in the world. I get up and shove through the lot of them, and they all laughing because they think I'm scared of them and their wedding bells.

I know the rules. He'll give me a chance to get going.

I run, and him soon after. I run like hell to show him what a good sprinter I am, to show him only someone really fast could maybe catch up, not like the snot-lads racing behind him pushing and pulling each other. I run towards the gate into the field, looking back to make sure he's still there. I run past the bicycle shed where the Travellers play and they all stop and look and cheer and I don't know which one of us they're cheering for. I leap over the gate and into the field because, if he's going to catch me, that's the best place. That's the plan I'd made, ready if this ever happened, ready for a long time now.

He's close. I'm trying to rub off the muck, he grabs me. I fall face forward, he falls right on top. Sebastian is right on top of me.

I lie there, face in the grass, not sure what to do, my heart nearly bouncing out, everything quiet like there is nothing else anywhere. The two of us. We lie together like that for a while, enough time to get the feel for it.

He says my name. I can't believe he says my name, just like that. He says it again. I turn to face him. The football lads are miles behind, stuck at the bike shed where the Travellers have stopped them for toll. The girls all still by the fuchsia, The Twins craning their necks to see what will happen next so they can tell each other and report to Gráinne.

The non-football lads are watching, hanging upside-down from the monkey bars.

I want to say his name back but nothing comes out except 'yeah'. I look at him and the truth is he's so lovely and I smile at the good of it and then we kiss, on the lips.

NYCTINASTY

Forty-five minutes before the call is due. Enough time for a bath. Henna's rinsed out, conditioner's in. So do it, as a kind of warm-up, a preamble of sorts. A cleansing of the soul. Fucking hell, listen to yourself.

Bea's nervous. Turning on the tap, she dribbles bath oil into the hot water and positions the phone. In case the call comes early. Not sure yet if it'll be a video call or not. Was this mentioned? Be ready for either. Or, stick tape over the phone's lens, say it's broken, say you don't know what's wrong with it.

The text appeared unexpectedly among her work notifications yesterday. She'd stared at the string of words, repeating them, trying to root out any hidden meaning. Should have changed his pet name back to a formal First name/Surname in her phone's Contacts a long time ago; looked stupid when it popped up with its familiar jauntiness, as if the last twenty-odd years hadn't slithered past without him. Change this before the day is over; complete at least this one act. Maybe delete the entire thing: texts, call history, his slick avatar. In youth from rock to rock I went / From hill to hill in discontent. Excrement. Malcontent. If the call comes early, don't answer, just text back. Do not mention you're in a bath. That it's already late morning here in New Zealand, that you're already thirteen hours into his Irish tomorrow. Text you're busy, sorry to have missed, you'll call back in five, in a few, you'll call back soon. Fuck, will it be video or voice? After all these years.

She goes to the bedroom to strip. From hill to hill in discontent / Of pleasure high and turbulent. Two old His 'n' Hers Easter Rabbit costumes on hangers hooked over her wardrobe door. Laptop lying dead on the bed. She placed it there earlier to remind herself to charge it so she could finish the evaluations. She'd promised her creative writing students she'd have their assignments graded and back in their inboxes, complete with critique, by today. Why make promises you know you'll struggle to keep. Of pleasure high and turbulent / Most pleased when most uneasy. Sleazy, Queasy.

At least she has only one left to grade. She doesn't want to send any of them back until they're all graded, knowing how college students are, how they'd judge her depending on the order in which she completed each submission, how they'd read into every little slip-up, every suggestion of favouritism. She has of course kept her favourite 'til last, a piece detailing the sequence of events in the dissolution of a relationship (the student had used the word 'unravelling' in their initial proposal, and she'd explained that this word may mean the exact opposite of what was presumably intended, that to unravel generally means to solve or untangle). Plugs the laptop in, leaves it bleeping red by the bedside, turns to the costumes.

She drapes the larger Easter rabbit arms over the hanger-shoulders of the smaller. She lays the coupled faux-fur costumes on her bed. She places a tube of lipstick on the bleeping laptop so she'll remember to apply it later, and heads back into the bathroom.

She doesn't usually wear lipstick, most shades clash with her hennaed hair, both colours emphasizing each other's artifice. Maybe she should just let her hair go grey, just let it go. She bought the shiny bullet-shaped lipstick in a giddy scramble through city centre yesterday (it's named Starlet Vixen, how could she not). Now the buy-rush feels moronic. After all these. Anyway, he's older too. What would he look like now.

Stepping into the bath, she twists the gushing water off, switches on the jets. She sits centred in the loud heat, holding her knees tight to her chest. The dog patters in (had she not put him out on the bedroom's narrow metal balcony where he can gaze over at the parrot in the apartment across the street, had she not put him out and closed the door to his whining). Drops onto his belly with a grunt, lays head between paws, sighs. She sighs too. It feels good. She sighs again, louder, with a kind of growl at the end. His ears cock, bristly brows see-sawing. She registers anxiety in them both, begins to feel her blood throbbing. First her head, then bolting to her wrists, ankles. How Love Fled. Should have taken more Solpadeine. Maybe she did. Don't worry little dog, everything is fine. Wanna see your birdy-buddy later? Wanna go walkies? From shore to shore in excrement.

The oily surface is breaking in furious whorls. Relax. She raises an arm, watches water snake down over the tiny indigo wings of a tattooed swift, down down along a tetchy vein. She'd bought the bath oil after the lipstick, imagining herself exactly as she is now; cocooned by sweet heat, wall clock ticking behind the drone of fizz, her phone, propped on the laundry basket, warbling notifications to itself in its own language. Check it? Nah, it'll be just her neighbourhood WhatsApp group discussing bin-collection disappointments, or her Faculty of Literature colleagues posting memes which she won't understand but will heart anyway. What if there's no fucking call from him at all? Or he texts instead?

– Sorry Bea mistake take care
– Sorry wrong number
– ha!!! butt call! apolojeez
(hope all good w/you)
– Butterfingers SOZ 😵

Shut down the phone, let the whole bastarding thing die.

No. Do not let it die.

Switching off the jets, she unfurls pinkened limbs. Calm down, what the hell is wrong with you. Reaches between her legs, closes her eyes so she won't see the dog, rubs her clitoris till climax. In the heightened after-glow bliss, an article she read recently on the female orgasm surfaces; the uterine contractions of orgasm are designed to vacuum seminal fluid deposited in the vagina up past the threshold of the cervix and into the waiting uterus to enable fertilization. Vacuum, deposited, threshold, waiting. Picturing oily bathwater swirling around in her egg-less womb, she tunes in to the post-orgasmic whoosh whoosh pulsing in her ears, and wills her blood to settle.

Think back, twenty-three years ago. Walk through it.

Three in the morning, Spring drizzle, we're driving home to Galway city from the staff costume party in Connemara. There's a half-moon glazing the road with light. We're both drunk. Passing the entrance to Silver Strand, I remember the car beams catching two small white discs (knee-height?) shining out at us from the hedgerow then gone in a flash. We decide to pull in, stretch our legs, get some air, look at the sea, sober up a bit. I forget whose idea it was. It was mine. The rabbit heads of our costumes hanging limp down our backs, we sit on the damp dunes and listen to a fox calling out from a field behind us (let it be a vixen? calling out to her mate?) I said it sounds beautiful, he said it's sad or some similar belligerent word.

We can see her, in the distance, a shrieking shape greyed against the darker field. Sheltering the vixen, a blanket of sleeping ox-eye daisies have their petals closed. Yes, I know flowers don't actually sleep. I'm going to be lyrical with this scroll-back, I'm going to allow for it. Choose to picture their pale flower heads fastened neat like daintily pursed lips, or tiny clenched fists, depending on your present bearings. Imagine them waiting till dawn, when they'll open with a score inscribed for whoever wants to count out their skinny little petals, which is no one (we'll both be long long gone). To love/love not, that is the scoop each ox-eye holds sealed inside tonight. Let them.

Remember the fox, spotting us, taking us in, then fleeing across the field, the lanky daisies swaying sodden in her wake. We turn our faces to the sea. The earlier alcohol is a shadowy cloak slipping off these our faux-fur shoulders. The sea, wide awake, reaches in. There's no fading darkness, there's no approaching dawn. We are here, stalled, neither coming nor going.

Twenty years' difference between us. We've spent the past three together. We got matching tattoos after the first year; tiny swifts in flight, one on his left wrist, one on my right, yes it was my first birthday gift to him, a surprise, one he was too polite or maybe too foolhardy to refuse, yes I didn't tell him I was getting one too on the day I walked him into the tattoo parlour, yes it was so the pair of swifts could appear linked when we held hands, yes I knew there was humiliation attached with such branding but the humiliation was different for each of us. My swift had always looked smudged and uncertain compared to the hyper-sharp indigo lines on his young skin.

I look at him. I want him to look back. He doesn't. The hollow V at the base of his throat heaves as he swallows, swallows what, swallows air, swallows maybe spit, a thin cough, some flimsy milk-and-water words. I know they're coming, these faithless fucking words. I fasten my arms around his shoulders, listen to the sea rumble over its own blunt pebbles; the well-worn intimacy of it. A shallow tide tonight, it's nearly in, it will go back out, was all this really a giant lumbering old pendulum.

He's fidgety. Rolling his shoulders away from me, he says he needs to move his limbs, pins and needles, then a joke about voodoo dolls I don't understand. Stripping, we ball our costumes in a rabbit-fuzz jumble on the sand and walk towards the neap tide. When its pearly-grey waters whisper (yes, I saw pearls, I heard them roll), when they whisper grey around our ankles, we keep walking, walking, out into the night sea. The water feels the same as the air though occasional small currents of coldness or warmth glide around our legs, pushing and pulling, go back, go forward, stay where you are. Still we walk on.

When the water comes up to our armpits (remember that chill, didn't we cross a kind of threshold then), we decide to lie floating on our backs, splay our limbs. Picture the waves rocking us drowsy, spinning our bodies slow like clocks out of sync. I was one tick-tock behind, one blink trailing blind, I knew that, even then. He starts to whistle. I think I find his hand. (I think I want to forgive.)

Imagine in such a place closing your eyes because you want to fix it there, always there for retrieval night or day, a story you tell yourself, some small details amended, imagine thinking ahead like that, thinking these silver-tipped waves could be captured solid, the cross-section of an instant and the trap slams shut, opening to a white limestone sculpture of water glistening on a pedestal years from now on the other side of the world.

We were heedless of the few scrappy stars winding around that night's moon, and each of them heedless of us below, of whether it's morning, noon, night, of what's past or what's to come for us, for the fox, the tight-lipped flowers, the whole sorry lot of us. The water that held us was shifting. Always ahead of itself, stretching up into every ragged shore.

And still we floated, and he was still whistling, and we were now a little further out. Ribbons of gummy seaweed had begun to wrap around ankles, around wrists. For once, I didn't think about spiny sea urchins, stinging jellyfish, basking sharks, drownings, disasters. I just spun gentle, listening to his whistle, thinking of the sea floor as a soft palm and us a pair of dice rolling around within its lines, beneath a waning, a semicircular, a half-there moon.

Eyes closed falling asleep to wake in exactly the same place the same after these twenty-odd years all clocks stopped (but this whine, God, this small whine) all eyes all lips remaining shut all eyes remaining perfect orbs rolling snug in their dark their oily sockets.

There is no. Fuck. Shut up.

And lay here exposed until the bathwater turns cold until this grimy veil of bath oil in dregs on these my exposed limbs these mauve exposed, to expose that there's no, until the whine of the dog, did you feed the dog, until his stupid whine finally breaks through.

Open the balcony doors for the poor creature. Go outside with him.

There is, as you already know, no call due.

She stands naked on the balcony behind her dog as he barks across at the parrot who she suspects is nothing more than a feathered fake in an ornamental cage. She waits, lets Auckland's noon air numb her damp skin. Finally, wrapping a towel around her, she sinks down in a corner of the metal balcony and goes back to that spring night in Connemara, and deeper down to the dawn that followed.

A half-empty moon, a pair of dice, still we are here in the night sea at Silver Strand, floating with eyes closed, limbs splayed, holding hands I think. Waves are spinning us slow in our cradle, yes the waves are hands rocking, yes the soft seabed an open palm, all that.

The fox yelps again, but this time her call seems so far away it doesn't exist, at least not here, not at this wide time we are in together.

I open my eyes. We have drifted far offshore. The outgoing tide. Or are we caught in a rip tide? Fuck. Letting go of you, I drop my legs, try to touch the sea floor with my toes. No floor. Nothing but ropes of floating seaweed. What?

I lurch forward, sink down. God, no. Thrashing, my body falls sideways, falls back. Our limbs strike underwater. Strike again. No. I try to raise my head above the waves, hair in my eyes, fuck, hair sucked thick into my mouth, waves plashing over my head, no, push my face up, breathe, try to shout your name, limbs clobbering, head pushed back underwater, no, are we going to drown, no God no

A window swings open in the apartment block across the way; a snappy young newsreader conjures weather-forecast tones. *Mild, partly cloudy, with a small chance of localized showers for the rest of the afternoon, 19 degrees, 68 per cent humidity, wind coming in off the coast at 16 km an hour.*

It's cold on the balcony. The hair conditioner has hardened on her head, her bare soles press against the metal mesh. The dog leans against her (did I feed him) (when did he last get a walk) and she realizes she's shivering. She draws him close, I'm sorry, wraps him inside the towel with her. He looks up, looks away when she catches his eye. Maybe the why of that Connemara night, the why it couldn't have turned out any differently no matter what. Maybe one of the whys.

The Easter costume party, at the department head's house in Connemara. Mid-term break. Most of the staff from the School of English, people dressed up as rabbits or chickens.

As a result of staff shortages at the start of term, he'd been quickly hired (with her backing) as a temporary assistant tutor. It was a fixed-term, one-semester-only contract, for the Contemporary Irish Poetry module. By mid-term, they both knew it was not going to be renewed; he was not performing well, did not have enough understanding of the subject, or of the art of teaching. Couldn't cross that bridge from student to teacher. So, this was his first ever faculty party, and likely his last. More importantly, at least to her, this was the first time the two of them could be together, openly, in front of her colleagues (*their* colleagues now, he said, ha ha).

Ever since she'd joined the faculty years prior, she'd been surprised to note that it appeared she was going to be granted special leverage, a dispensation of sorts on any behaviour normally deemed inappropriate, a special dispensation on account of her status not only as foreigner, but as highly qualified female foreigner. Somehow, the bending of the rules seemed to be expected from the likes of her, a solitary woman who'd upped and left her homeland to travel across to the other side of the globe, to exactly the other side of the globe (that part was important), for no reason other than a wish to 'get *out* there', as she'd explained to them.

The majority of her colleagues already knew what had been going on for most of the three years of his undergraduate degree, but the Easter costume party was the first time people didn't have to pretend not to know. There was collective relief, a threshold had been safely crossed, a drawbridge pulled.

God he was so nervous that night, the night of the party. Well, nervous at the beginning, when we first pulled up in his old Nissan Micra. That fucking car. He wanted to be seen to be the one driving it, imagine thinking that THAT was going to secure his standing, a dirty old car his parents gave him as a graduation present. I said nothing. It was nearly endearing, this childlike angst amongst what were now, at least for the next few months, his fucking PEERS (as I kept reminding him). Nearly charming, except he got so, he got SO bastarding drunk. A lot more than, much much more than me. An angry drunk, that's a good phrase, angry, angry with who, with himself for being, is it for being drunk. Angry for being drunk, or drunk for being angry, and, tell me, how can you tackle that. You can't. I'd NEVER seen him so, I swear, I'd never ever.

Look, it was the stupid Wordsworth poem, I love that poem, he knows I love that poem, it's not a popular poem but this is my fucking thing and that's my favourite poem, he couldn't, he wouldn't quote the words right, I know it's not the most serious thing in the world, I know, the, it's *from hill to hill* not *from shore to shore*, you daft, you, you DAFT idiot, we covered it! Remember! The English Romantic Age, last year's module, final semester, come on now, you remember.

He said nobody cares, apparently nobody cares if you change the words, sorry, I care, I said, it's William Wordsworth and I bloody care, the words are *from hill to hill*, not *shore to shore*, get it right if you're going to / Shut up, Bea, nobody actually cares, look around, we're all fluffy Easter rabbits here or big yellow fucking chickens, having a few drinks, smoking a few blunts, just having a laugh, having / Calm down, no need to get angry, it's, the line is *hill to hill*, that's all that's / Jesus Christ it doesn't actually matter, you're being fucking stupid in front of / If it doesn't matter why are you saying *shore to shore*, you git, if it apparently doesn't matter, if apparently according to YOU no one cares, why are you so / Shut up Bea, you've no idea how little I care, you've no, you're embarassing yourself, you're fucking embarassing, you're a total embarassment / That's, that's not, calm the fuck down, it's just a poem, calm down please, it's, so why don't you give us one of YOUR cute little poems, Bunny, one of your special / Stop, you're being a real shit, why are you policing everything like Sergeant Major Arsehole, can you hear yourself *calm down calm down calm down calm* quit acting the big fucking mammy, I've enough of this horseshit, get your / Bunny, just STOP this, God, just / No, forget it, we're going home, get your / Look, I was only, sorry but words actually matter, it's an important poem, of course they matter / Swear to fuck it matters to no one but you here tonight, Bea. Come on. I'm finished. We're going.

Remember he let me drive his car home, that was something. Like he'd thrown in the towel on this whole Big Man thing. Look, I was drunk too, stop implying otherwise. Just, he was drunker, one step ahead off track out of step. The row in the car, him clamming up like a big baby, a big drunk stoned bunny-rabbit baby sitting there furry arms folded. You're being really pathetic, Bunny, yes, immature, belligerent and pathetic, snap out of it, you spineless git.

I've called him Bunny from the day we met, I don't know why, he doesn't look anything like a cute bunny, maybe that's the why, also because I know he doesn't like it, which is funny, Bunny, and when the costume party invite came it was perfect; be a chicken! be a rabbit! so I bought the two Easter Bunny costumes, and he thought it was funny too.

And here he is, Guinness splattered down the shiny white fur. Of course it's embarrassing. Did he think he was right or did he not want to be wrong. Just say you're wrong. Words are important. If you know something, say it. I know my Wordsworth, don't pick a fight about Wordsworth for fuck's sake. If he hadn't insisted on reciting it wrong. Recite it, yes, but recite it correctly please as it was written please no freestyle deconstruction interpretation fragmentation word-collage found-poem hybrid erasure bitchery thank you fuck off back to your mammy with that nonsense. Or, you know, you could just shut up. Sorry but it's true. How would you like it if someone recited one of your poems wrong. Maybe you'd like that. Cutting edge. Big Man at the party, not a word out of him when it matters. Just pins, needles and arms-fold silence. Big Bunny Rabbit Baby, speak!

So, perhaps a result of alcohol, perhaps a memory lapse, perhaps he actually believed they were the words. They were not. Yes, as I drove, I recited the poem for him, beginning to end, maybe not such a great idea, maybe not my best moment. Just get home, is all he said.

No. I didn't want us to go back to the city, go to bed, put flabby distance between the now with these wrong words and the what was to come if, the with all due respect Bea, the we were both a bit, to be fair, to be honest, the let's give each other a bit of, a bit of what Bunny, a bit of space Bea, a bit of fucking space.

And that is why I pulled in to Silver Strand, why I asked him to sit with me by the sea for a while, so we could sober up, take a breath, talk it over, get to the bottom, whatever. I said if we both are seeing double then the half-moon will become one full one, just for us. So, this is what it was: it was a wrongly recollected poem, alcohol and a rip tide.

Go on then, get to dark dawn.

Here we are. We are drowning together in the black Atlantic night, slowly and without a word between us. Maybe this is it, what's to come. Maybe this is the final what now to the ghost.

My limbs are burning from the constant flailing, my throat stings, my lungs ache. We are far out at sea, the shore a distant thin line, translucent when we can see it through the slapping waves. I stop the stupid thrashing, give in to the multitude of currents around us, focus on just keeping my chin above water. You are still struggling beside me. Sucking air in through tight lips, I grasp your hand, draw you to me. I hold my breath as my body sinks, adjusting to your weight. You were always the better swimmer but, God, look at you now. You have no strength, a rag doll, unravelling. You are so much worse than me. How your helplessness stirs something. I will not leave you. I will bring us to the other side of this.

Trying to right myself in the water, I start treading my legs, right left pause right left, my arms around you. You are squeezing me too hard, mouth clenched, your limbs sliding down my body. I tell you, small breaths, stop struggling. You do as you're told. I am all you have.

I turn you around, place your back to me, put my arms around you, interlock my fingers over your chest. I tell you to stretch out your legs, bring in your arms, calm down, calm it all the way down, I will tread for the both of us and, when we are out of the currents, I will try to swim us to shore.

And so we drift, the undercurrents pushing and pulling us further into the cold Atlantic. If there is a wild horizon out there, it is unseeable. Lying on my back, I carry you face up on my breast like a child, holding your chin in my hand, picturing you eyeing the fuzzy half-moon. You are heavy, your torso hangs down between my splayed legs. Your arms exed across your chest, you are gripping me with both your hands (your nails embed and leave secret crescents that will take months to heal).

You are quiet. I watch your even, shallow breathing. I am waiting for the dark undertow to settle. I try to move in small circles, try to have some small control over the currents. I try to use the moon as anchor, try to keep an eye on the shore, that luminous, thin arc in the far distance I am not convinced is not some sort of diaphanous mirage.

And things appear eventually to fall into place, a kind of unreal settlement. You have given yourself over to me. Imagine. We steady as one into some kind of cold fixed rhythm, in out left right tick tock love love not. How long does this slippery alignment last. I can't seem to put a figure on it. We are bobbing together but we are getting nowhere.

You are becoming heavier, how is it that you are becoming heavier, this weight, is it trying to pull us down to the dicey open palm. Your wide chest rises and falls, rises and falls on me. And the hollow V on your throat, look, quiet as a mouse.

I am cold. I watch flickering aircraft pass overhead trailing their low rumble, heading west to America or east to Europe and beyond. Dear shifting pole stars, dear secret satellite systems in the sky, do you pull us in your chemical wakes, are we too heavy, are we a burden, which one is a burden, will we cancel each other out, this east west north south.

What are they, pinkish, are they bright streaks appearing ashore in the sky over that dark field of ox-eyes, look. Dawn doesn't come to us, we have to go to it. Or maybe will it meet me halfway. Are you mad don't ask for too much. I didn't ask for anything, I didn't ask for this did I. Dear God, I did not. All of the clueless useless people ashore, asleep warm inside houses, being ferried blind to their dawn without even the slightest show of gratitude. Lazy arseholes. Calm down. I am telling myself to calm down.

He's gurgling. Salt in the throat. I feel it. Salt soot burying in. Creep. Sweep. A scalded chimney. Don't think about it. This dirt. I feel the wet weight of his skull on my lungs. Stone. Put a stone in the bag, throw the bag of meowls in the water. Are you sleeping. I cannot see his face. I stare at the crown of his head. Dark strands of hair radiating out from a central spot, celestial white spot, a celestial ceiling, is this another thing, this tiny star of skin in the centre so pale smooth against his straggly black strands, wheeling outward, cosmos, is the tide still going out, what about that time in between when the tide stands still, listen, remember when you said to me, listen you need to hear this, Bunny, remember the time remember when you said, don't think of us as a long-term thing, when you said, I won't be hanging around here forever, Bea, get real, I was just, listen, soon as this semester's over, you said, as soon, I won't be tied, Bea, putting up with your, don't be so goddamned, you called me clingy, it's embarrassing, you said, it's fucking embarrassing, you said, are we tied at the hip or something, what is it you want Bunny, tell me now, space or time if you could have one of these, one in each pocket and, look! is this another thing, a blotchy star of whitest spiralling out into this his dark head, not going anywhere now Bunny are you, no, and why am I tied here at the hips to a deadweight bedraggled buoy with a galaxy for skin, a bag with a stone heart, a helpless, a useless arsehole, did I need to hear that, Bunny, did you need to say that back then, when words mattered, clinging to me now aren't you with your tight little rabbit soul, we're going, damn right we're going, every one of these scraggly black strings attached to the tide, the tide going out with all this shit or no, stop, no, is this a big black sea urchin here in the tide on my breast, yes the git, the spiny, spineful spinesome spineless, in the middle the round, urchin mouth one side, anus the other, am I looking at anus or mouth, what's the difference, both suns being ferried to the dawn without so much as a thank you, my lovely, my very own groaning burden, now come on now, you know I cannot swim us both there, swim to shore, from shore to shore, what do you expect from me, come on, get real, I am old so cold there is nothing here, my limbs are numb, nothing, where are my limbs, maybe your eyes are open, maybe not, maybe half, maybe one, are these other limbs, are your eyes open, oh God.

Bunny?

He mumbles something, then back to a low gurgle, a child, a huge suckling urchin. The stars are gone, wrong, not gone, just we can't see them any more, they're still there dithering, only hidden by the bright pink and orange blooms happening now, look, look! in laser streaks, rising in the sky yes from the east, oh these overland torches seeking out what, remember the car beams shining on those two white discs in the hedgerow back there knee-height remember then gone in a flash. In a flash. Blink. No looking back, just do it. What? I am too cold, I am too old. This dead water, how. A hard shivering cold. What was the voodoo doll joke, is it too late for that, is there a sting to those spikes. Oh yes, them there.

And the vixen calls out to me from the rosy the lonely shore has she been calling out for long and I know now what she is saying. You have to go to your dawn, it won't come to you. You have to leave the black sea urchin behind. All his hard spines, get them away from you. The sickle-marks. He doesn't belong deadweight on your breast. Leave him be. Give him to the Atlantic if it wants him that bad. Give him to the open palm waiting below if it wants him. And beneath the surface it's quiet, is it sleeping. A soft sea bed. Let the black sea urchin go. Let him go there. There below.

Say it now, Bea.

With one hand, I loosen his grip, it's easy. With my other, I circle a fistful of hair from the side of his black head. He rouses, too late for rousing. I push his head underwater, rolling away from him. There's no special noise, nothing much changes on the sea surface. After a time, how much time, not much, I let go. Did he touch me, did he reach out and touch my arm before he began to tick-tock away towards the dim west, out into his secret, his own chill, his very own sea.

My limbs are returned to me. I am light as air. I twist my back to the sky and swim slow a wide slow arc through the invisible arrows until yes in time I reach the brightening shore. The hard cold sand. Keep going. Find our jumble of rabbit costumes, pull mine on, hood up, wrap his around my arm, sand rasping skin, walk back past the oxeyes. Their flower heads are beginning to open. No thank you, Little Ox-eye, hold on to it. I'm going home.

I'm still cold when I get back to the house, my body hurts. I take a shower and sleep for a few hours. That evening, I return to the Department Head's house. I apologize about the previous night's unpleasantness, explain about the continued disagreement in the car after we left the party, he's such a hothead, you know the way he could the way he can be sometimes, stubborn as a child, yes his insistence on a solo swim, his demand to be left alone, what could I do, when he gets like that. And now, God, his unexplained disappearance. Did he, by any chance, return here? He actually told me to fuck off home, give him breathing space. Breathing space, can you believe it? Yes, over a silly poem, over a line in a poem. Oh God oh God, I'm getting a bad feeling about this, I'm getting a bad vibe. Look, if he turns up here, tell him he can take as much time and space as he needs, I only want to know he's safe, I only want to let him know he can come home when he's ready. I only ever wanted what was good for him. God, I swear, I'll kill him when I see him. What he put, what he puts me through! But I forgive him. Of course I forgive him. Tell him I forgave him if he turns up.

As I demonstrate my distress, they reassure me everything will be alright, it's not my fault, drink does strange things sometimes, he's unlikely to come back here, considering everything, maybe he's gone to a friend's, maybe it's all been a bit much for him, all the, it's a lot to take on, young lad like him. Maybe just give him some space. When he's ready, he'll make contact. Best to drop it, Bea. Go on home.

And four weeks later I read online about an eyeless, lipless, hairless body washing up further out west on Coral Strand, the grave-wax skin darkened, the little indigo swift gone (that somehow is the worst part). By then, I've quit the job and severed all contact with my former colleagues, I've sought out and accepted a part-time lecturing job back in New Zealand, I've left Galway to return home.

Yet, all these years, all this distance and you're still not gone, you're still clinging on.

She leaves the balcony, empties the bath, watches the spinning gurgle clockwise, ha! as the last of the bathwater drains away. Closing the balcony doors, she looks again at the parrot, is it alive or dead, is it real, what does it matter, the dog thinks it is. Oh God he's done his doggy-pee in the balcony corner, the edge of the towel sodden. It's leaked along the metal mesh and dripped down through the storeys, how many storeys, one two three four five not counting this one, it'll have disappeared by the time it gets to the fifth, as in, the first storey. Hope no one was out. They'd never trace it back to here anyway, enough of a distance between, and no provable connection, loads of people have dogs, accidents happen.

She walks back into the bedroom, he follows her. They plonk down together on either side of the coupled rabbit-costumes figure reclining on the bed, its faux-fur arms hugging its torso. Her laptop glows blue on the bedside table. Good, get that last submission done, then get all the critiqued pieces sent back out to the students by this afternoon.

But first, let's get this call out of the way. (Look oh look at him the shape of him inside my bunny costume inside his bunny costume lying here beside me!) Now my own delights I make. What. Apply Starlet Vixen, a little touch to your lips. And take the secret phone from the bunny's pocket. Okay, good. Lie back on the pillow, tell me what to type;

– Sorry Bea, got mixed up with
the time zones, what a f*cking dope !!
😍 will call tomorrow, thinking of you xx

and listen out now for the message received notification ping from the phone still propped on the laundry basket beside the bath.

I know none of this is good. I know. Most pleased when most uneasy.

When she hears the beautiful, the sharp ping hit in the bathroom, it's like a warm shot in the arm, it's like what she imagines a shot of heroin in the mangled arm of an addict would feel like. The vibrating ping causes the phone to fall off the laundry basket and clatter into the empty bath. As she drags the laptop onto her knee to finish the final critique, she sniggers at the overly romantic, unrefined metaphor of herself as forlorn addict. Ha ha ha! Pathetic. Like something one of the weaker students would write.

She'd given her Creative Writing class a simple brief: *1,500 words on a life-changing personal experience you've had. Note: it must contain some reference to a body of water*. She'll go easy with this final critique, but she'll be firm. This student (a favourite, it's true) is proving to be an interesting challenge; appearing to wilfully misunderstand suggestions, wilfully extract double meanings where the meaning is clear.

She'll start the feedback with a comment on the submission's title, 'ON DIVING INTO AN EMPTY POOL' (too abstract, one-dimensional, unfledged, a wasted opportunity, a parable-title is not always the sophisticated approach people think it is). She'll suggest something with greater clarity embedded, something that can carry weight, a metaphor from the physical world is always a good start, is there something in nature that maybe intrigues you, an animal, a plant, something you don't necessarily understand, something that could be used as a symbol of a deeper conflict, a type of diving board into your story.

ACKNOWLEDGEMENTS

I am wildly grateful to the following:
the team at Lilliput Press,
my agent Marianne Gunn O'Connor,
the Arts Council of Ireland and Leitrim County Council,
my pals from The Sandy Field Writers Group (especially its founder Una Mannion),
all the journals and magazines who have kindly published my work,
my colleagues on the Writing & Literature and the Performing Arts programmes at ATU Sligo,
the many crossed-path strangers whose words and actions have marked me,
my beloveds: Bernardine Hanratty, Cecily Gilligan, and soulmate Kirsten Mosher,
the cailleach,
and finally, and forever, my fine men, Comhall Cába and Finn Fíor.